GHOSTS

GHOSTS

MORIO KITA

Translated by
Dennis Keene

KODANSHA INTERNATIONAL
Tokyo • New York • London

Originally published by Bungei Shuto in 1954 under the title *Yūrei*.
Distributed in the United States by Kodansha America, Inc., 114 Fifth
Avenue, New York, N.Y. 10011, and in the United Kingdom and conti-
nental Europe by Kodansha Europe Ltd., Gillingham House, 38-44
Gillingham Street, London, SWIV IHU. Published by Kodansha
International Ltd., 17-14 Otowa 1-chome, Bunkyo-ku, Tokyo
112, and Kodansha America, Inc.

91 92 93 10 9 8 7 6 5 4 3 2 1

Library of Congress Cataloging-in-Publication Data
Kita, Morio, pseud.
    [Yūrei, English]
    Ghosts / by Morio Kita : Translated by Dennis Keene.
    p.   cm.
    translation of: Yūrei.
    ISBN 4-7700-1559-3
    I. Title.
PL855.I65Y813 1991
895.6'35–dc20   91-36086

GHOSTS

1

Why this desire to relate what we recall of the past? Because, just as any race has its mythology, so an individual bears within him his own private myths, myths which also gradually fade, finally disappearing into the depths of time; and yet things leave their traces, events of the vague and distant past having found their way into the heart, and these things concern us through the years, are a constant preoccupation of the deeper reaches of the mind, lasting until that time when all our actions cease. And suddenly one day this usually unconscious activity may open up for us, become an awakening of sorts; much like a silkworm, as it slowly eats away a mulberry leaf for no reason it can comprehend, becoming conscious of the slight sound its own mastication makes. So it raises its head, unsure, fearful almost as it gazes around its world, experiencing itself as something ... whatever that might be.

* * *

Mother spent her early years abroad. I have no idea how she came to know my father. In her room there was a large mirror, as wide as a door, of clear glass in a carved frame of dark, lustrous wood, something totally out of place in a Japanese-style room. Since there was nowhere to fit the thing it was allowed to lean against one of the walls, whence it seemed to be sulkily scrutinizing the other furnishings. As if to cheer the mirror up, my mother made every effort to have the rest of the room conform to Western taste, concealing all the tatami under a gray carpet and placing a bed, a cupboard, and so on wherever seemed appropriate, creating, to my innocent eyes, a room of perfect elegance, one worthy of a fairy tale, with her clothes—soft, voluminous, with frilly sleeves, a riot of color—cast over a chair; the Gobelin tapestry which covered one of the walls; and all the other yards of cloth she used to hide the plain, the threadbare, and the trite.

I loved that room when I was small, not simply, I think, because it aroused my curiosity, but because its alienness appealed to some desire in me for the unaccustomed, for what my skin had not grown used to. That solid mahogany dressing table, for example, contained within its shadows something guaranteed to entice an innocent mind, as did the contents of its drawers, the brushes, the nail varnish, and all the tools of her toilette, which stirred a deep wonder in me, much as when I used to discover, later on in childhood, some rare insect or mushroom in the woods. No less intriguing were those tiny bottles of skin lotion and perfume, the heavy aroma about them which made one's skin creep, and the scent spray of cut glass with such a charming little rubber ball on top that I longed to have one of my own. I would grasp the scent spray in both hands and, absorbed by its precise, elaborate glitter, start to lose all awareness of the passing of time, until suddenly I sensed the mirror was watching me, its cold face apprehending every move I made. For a moment I would be startled, feeling a strong urge to run away, but the cowardly impulse soon vanished, to be replaced by a slight sense of concern, of expectation even, that something might be about to appear there in the mirror momentarily, some face, perhaps some shape, not mine but of another.

Certain shapes fascinated me, quite why I am not sure, but I know I would often squat down on the carpet and speculate about the white pattern dyed into it. There were branches and leaves, human forms in various postures, and yet if one moved a little way back then the branches and leaves and people seemed to merge into each other, producing what appeared to be a face, not unlike like that of the Sphinx in the tapestry on the wall; and yet abruptly that too would grow confused again, the pattern break and the face disappear, as my eyes lost their magic focus and the dull disorder of what was there before took over. I would spend hours staring at the carpet, ruminating on this face in all its transformations, confident that eventually its rich, Protean actuality would reveal itself; but to the last it remained ambiguous, leaving each time a sense of disappointment, the feeling that I had been fulfilled in some desire only to be deceived.

Once, and one time only, I asked my mother about the face, in a voice I'd meant to sound casual but which burst out like a stifled cough.

"Face? What face? These are birds, aren't they? And these

are leaves. There aren't any faces, are there?"

As she said this the face did in fact disappear, and even the shapes that I'd firmly believed to be those of people turned into what I saw they truly were, those of birds. I thought she must have used some kind of magic, and when I looked up into her own smiling face with its prominent white forehead, it seemed oddly to belong to someone I didn't know. I looked down again and moved my hand across the carpet, as if I were stroking the fur of some living creature.

Father seemed to be some sort of scholar; or at least I believed so for a long while until I gained some understanding of the world. Now I can see he was only a kind of high-class dilettante, someone of whom perhaps it could be said that he had understood only too well not just the glory but the petty meanness of the creative life he led, and this, combined with a longing for the satisfactions of the simple everyday, had meant he had finally committed himself to neither. So his coolheaded attachment to life resulted in a few books of travel and reminiscences, some essays, and one slim blue volume of poetry. No doubt the title of art critic or essayist would have been preferred, but he does seem to have been more noted as a travel writer.

When I was still quite small his hair was already turning gray. He wore square, rimless glasses for writing, and he was always forgetting where he'd left them. Whenever this happened the whole household would be turned upside down, as my mother, then the maid, and even our old nanny joined in the hunt, bustling about from room to room, not so much as if they were actually looking for something but as if their basic aim was merely to bustle. I would hurry along with everybody else, but something would usually distract me—a stain on the wall, or the shadow a tree in the garden cast upon the corridor—and I quite forgot what we were supposed to be searching for. Meanwhile the glasses themselves would turn up, on a tea table or under a cushion, even sometimes in the lavatory, and each time he would give a brief cry, followed promptly by a scowl, as he accepted the lost object from whoever had found it. This made everybody smile, and our nanny would burst into a fit of coughing as she tried to stifle the laughter behind her toothless gums.

Father didn't talk very much; indeed sometimes when I heard him make some remark it was like hearing a person's voice for the first time. He had the habit of raising his hand to his mouth as if he were about to cough, yet the cough itself seldom materialized. I can manage a certain hazy recall of this gesture, but am quite unable to summon up any image of his face, probably because a photograph I have of him when young has imposed itself on a much vaguer recollection of the face I really knew, and thus confused it. What does remain clear is my impression of the peculiar aura of silence that seemed to surround him. This silence was not the sense of restfulness, of peace, evoked by someone who has deliberately withdrawn from the world, like a recluse or a research scientist, but was more a feeling of weariness, of just not caring, much like, I suppose, the mood of a patient who is soon going to die, but with no suffering, no struggle.

Despite this, whenever my father was occupied in researching or writing something, he went about it with such singleminded purpose that to a child like me it was almost frightening. He would shut himself up in the living room and refuse to come out for meals, drag down a dozen books from the library shelves and open them, then drag down a few more and rummage through their pages. He behaved like someone, not studying, but struggling in the grip of some awful spell. I still find it hard to believe

5

that he was in fact doing something he enjoyed.

He had a small Japanese-style room, with an old-fashioned desk placed by the window, where he would squat, absurdly curled up, and cover reams of paper with his meticulous handwriting. He wrote with a brush, from time to time briskly scraping away at his ink block, which he always did in a diagonal way rather than the normal straight up and down. Inevitably there would be heaps of opened books scattered all around him, giving the impression that they, rather than my father, were the principal occupants of the room.

There were certainly plenty of books; in fact to say the house was buried in them would be no overstatement. He was an obsessive collector of almost any kind of book, and even the guest parlor was jammed with shelves on which they were arranged in no sort of order, ponderous specialist volumes side by side with children's books and women's literature that somebody had given him. Still, the place where they really ran riot was next door to the living room, in a room fifteen feet square with a high ceiling; here the shelves were lined up as in a public library, so close together you had to squeeze your way between them. Even that did not provide adequate space for all his books, however, and there were still lots piled on the floor. Since there were so many of them assembled in such force, it appeared that the books had developed an exaggerated idea of their own importance. This wasn't a question of what the value of any individual volume might be, since the fact of personal identity meant little in terms of this close-packed mob, this hard face of books turned silently toward the world without the least expectation apparently of ever being read. Nor did this neglect seem to bother them, for they had long ceased to rely on the possibility of any human intervention, being content to fall back into a more and more obstinate silence, an accumulation of pride buried under dust.

Thus it was a quite different attraction from that of my mother's which drew me to this room. I would climb the stairs, and there was my mother's room on the right, and to the left a small passageway which ended at the door to the library. When you turned the knob it just revolved pointlessly, as if the door had never once been opened nor ever would be, though it only felt like that because you didn't have to turn it: a push was all it needed. I would slip in as quietly as I could, but even so the floor made an awesome, rusty creaking, at which all the books would seem to prick up their ears, staring suspiciously in my direction to find out what sort of person had come in. There was one fat dictionary on a shelf immediately to the left which I was sure was really scrutinizing me, but every time I darted a searching look toward it it had already assumed again an expression of indifference. And yet, after these first few awkward moments, the books seemed to lose interest in me, for I no longer felt I was the object of their vigilance. I would wander about between the shelves, loitering occasionally to draw with my finger in the thin layer of dust. And among these books I also observed faces, various faces, as the red, blue, leather or paper bindings with the lettering on their spines created different features ... though, like the face in the carpet, these also vanished as soon as they were looked at closely.

There was one other room I should mention, and that was the parlor next to the hall. It was a peculiarly elaborate room, with an atmosphere not so much of the elegant as of the slightly disreputable, even of ill fame. The walls were done in a faded pink and the windows were covered by thick, double curtains, giving a sense of overdecoration, of artificiality, such as one would expect to find in the witches' palace in a fairy tale. When the lights were switched off at night, the curtains kept out even the faint light of the stars, leaving only an impenetrable, terrifying darkness.

Yet Mother often invited guests to our house, and when the lights went on in this room she looked extraordinarily foreign in their brilliant glare, more remote from everyday Japanese reality than the actual foreigners who were sometimes present. She would move among her guests, bestowing a few words here, a peal of radiant laughter there, and I would gaze at her, at her unruffled elegance and poise, wondering at the sight yet pleased with it as well. Once, I discovered an empty glass with a red cherry in it, but as soon as I took hold of the cherry, my lynx-eyed mother noticed and, seizing my hand with the cherry still clasped in it, slapped me playfully on the cheek. This amused everybody, one very ancient foreigner feeling called upon to stand up and address some friendly words to me in a Japanese I found totally incomprehensible; but all I experienced was a powerful sense of growing very small, no doubt from a feeling of shame both at being in a place that wasn't meant for me and allowing myself to be caught in such a situation. I went stiff all over, wishing I could vanish in a puff of smoke.

Yet I still went on sitting there. I knew that nobody was interested in me really, but it was nice even just sitting on a chair in the corner, hearing the talk and laughter of the guests and the tinkling of glasses, listening to a deliciously lazy melody issuing from the imposing, box-shaped gramophone. Whenever Mother changed a record it was always this one she chose, the call of a distant flute inviting one into a world quite different from our own, and as I listened I began to imagine that all that surrounded me, the room itself, the heavy curtains, the wooden dolls arranged on a shelf, had suddenly acquired an aura of intimacy, was no longer alien but something into which I could be absorbed, become a living part of. But that was only a momentary illusion, vanishing almost as soon as it came, and I would fidget awkwardly, hearing once more the cheerful conversations that had nothing to do with me.

This was the main reason why I was so envious of my sister. She was two years older than me and, being a child who took exactly after her mother, had no difficulty in being accepted in an environment from which I felt excluded. Whether she was being dandled on someone's knee, or merely sitting alone on a chair like me, she still clearly belonged to a world that was always beyond my reach, as if she were made, both body and soul, of quite different stuff from myself. Sometimes the grown-ups would move the table to one side of the room in order to dance, and she would always join in, while the guests were always glad to let her do so, dancing with her even if she could only manage the incompetent steps of a child.

When my cousin, who was the same age as my sister, came to play with us, the two of them would often imitate the grown-ups dancing. My cousin was a born actor and, bowing with impeccable aplomb, he'd take her hand and sweep her once around the floor, then throw his head back and produce a large guffaw, which made my sister look shyly down and giggle. Watching them, I used to laugh as well, but in an idiotic, unreal way, as I was always only a looker-on, and no matter how eager I was to have a go, whenever I asked they merely shook their heads. I suppose I realized, too, that for someone like me it was simply out of the question.

There was a game we'd made up, a combination of hide-and-seek and blindman's buff, which we always played in the parlor when my cousin was staying at our house. With the witches' palace now in total darkness you couldn't see anyone even if he was right in front of your nose, and we were all terrified of the dark anyway, so it wasn't so much a game we were involved in as an intense and nerve-racking way of experiencing the passing of time. However much you strained your eyes, everything was a uniform, inky black, a blackness which flowed unsparingly into the eyes until your whole body and the darkness merged and you could no longer work out where you ended and your surroundings began. Crouched down behind a chair, I would become anxious about this and start feeling my arms and legs to make sure I was still me, until at some point I'd be aware of the pursuer's slow approach. There would be a slight rustling, or a sense that a breath had traversed the dark, and as I started to edge cautiously away I sometimes found myself suddenly bumping right into the enemy, although this seldom prevented me making my escape, pressed flat against the wall in a corner. Yet whenever a hand brushed against my cheek in the dark, or when I was in pursuit and my own tentative fingers touched the nape of someone's neck, it produced a sensation which even now I am unable to describe satisfactorily; but it was as if the skin had become extremely thin, so that all physical sensations had come to the surface of the body, and thus the lightest of touches could produce a trembling throughout one's being. It was similar perhaps to something I shall describe later on, the excitement I was to feel in the silvery glitter of the dust on a butterfly's wings; even to one's first passionate contact with a woman's body.

When someone was caught the lights were turned on, and my sister would inevitably poke her head out from her hiding place and say how scared she'd been. If she was the one who was caught, she always gave a little shriek. But if she was chosen to find the other two, she would make such a noise and giggle so much she could never catch anybody, so someone else had to take over. My cousin, though, was the very opposite, and when he was "it" the game became deadly serious, for he made not the slightest sound, hardly even seeming to breathe as he stood quite still in the darkness, straining his ears and sniffing out his prey, toward whom he would make his stealthy, relentless way. The suspense was unbearable, and as I crouched in fear behind the sofa I experienced the illusion that my body had suddenly dissolved, become now totally absorbed into the pitch-darkness.

There was also the weight of that darkness, the way it moved; for the air in it was quite different from that of daylight, having a living quality one could feel on one's skin. The darkness tickled my ears, it crept slowly down my arms.

* * *

We tend to think of early childhood as a period of simple innocence, but this is merely another aspect of the inescapable process of forgetfulness. The reasons why we should forget are rarely scrutinized, and no doubt the principal one is that we choose deliberately to falsify the feelings of that time....

A light mist covered everything, so it was still early morning, and we were going to look for mushrooms. The maid took me to a large, open field where we walked among the thick, tall grass. The grass was so high that whenever I disturbed a drop of dew it fell hugely to the ground, like a large, soft ground-cherry. The sky was still hazed over, its light vague and unreal, and the wide expanse of grass seemed to stretch on forever, soaked in the dew, producing a unique odor which, as I breathed it in with all the dampness of the air, made me feel an inexplicable delight, combined with an equally indescribable sense of weariness that was enjoyable all the same, a clear apprehension of the freshness of the day. Among the stalks and leaves of grass were innumerable spiders' webs, transformed into lace hangings by the dew, and cuckoo spit, which did look exactly as if somebody had smeared the stems with spittle. And then I noticed, squirming about on a jagged leaf right in front of me, the most mysterious-looking insects, so odd one could hardly think of them as mere worms. I picked them up eagerly, one by one, dropping them into the empty bottle that the maid carried, an ordinary bottle of nontransparent amber glass. I still can't adequately describe the joy I felt, however, when my fingers touched what looked like a blob of spit and out crawled an insect with red and black stripes on its back, for it was as if I had discovered the hidden spirit of that particular piece of grass, a minor nymph or dryad. This wasn't like simply hearing sometime or other that gods are supposed to have inhabited the woods in former ages, but a knowledge at that early stage in life that they still did, because here was one of them.

So we returned home with the bottle stuffed with treasures, I looking back occasionally to make sure it was still safely in the maid's hand. But when we arrived and I laid the bottle on its side on the stone floor of the hall, my disappointment was enormous, for out from the thin neck of the bottle crept grass spiders and mantis larvae, dragging their damaged limbs, and gone without a trace was all the brilliance, the allure of life they had possessed among the field's damp grass. Then one gray spider came stumbling right toward my foot and I leaped back in alarm, so that the bottle rolled over and over across the floor; and out of its mouth came my spirit of the grass, a froghopper still in the larval stage yet also still brilliant in its red stripes, and that one moment seemed to compensate for all the disappointment I had just experienced, so clear and vivid did it seem. It was then, I think, that I first acquired the fascination with color that still remains with me.

Yet that field, only a hundred yards away from our house, eventually became something ordinary to me, something known. I learned to distinguish between those stalks which oozed a yellow liquid when broken and those which were naturally segmented, like the joints of my fingers; between those leaves covered with soft hairs and those which stung with needle sharpness. I understood that the bushes there were only clumps of grass, and that the possibility of my observing something still unknown beneath them had gradually disappeared. The various insects I discovered afterward were only ones whose forms had already been tucked away somewhere in my mind.

In one corner of the field remained the outer walls of some brick building that had been abandoned. Red pieces of broken brick were buried here and there in the ground, and a heap of whitish gray fragments of hewn stone lay scattered in one part. The maid used to take my sister and me there quite often, and we would play at housekeeping. Two stones rubbed together made a fine powder, and when enough had accumulated on a leaf, we'd offer it to each other as food. It was difficult to achieve the right combination of white powder and red brick dust, so sometimes I had to mix in some reddish earth as well; but, with my liking for the color red, I always seemed to add too much of it.

The most striking instances of redness in the field were the swarms of dragonflies when summer ended, and as the season deepened into autumn their undersides would turn a pure crimson, sparkling in the sky above the field as they spread their wings and soared, or perched on the iron railings that separated it from the cemetery. Boys much older than me would race after them with nets and sticks, while I would stand holding the maid's hand, watching with bated breath, hoping against hope that none of them would be caught. I suppose it was nothing more than jealousy on my part, for I was much too small and inept to be able to do anything like that myself.

From the far side of the field stretched endlessly away the desolate gloom of the cemetery, as far as the army barracks whose buildings one could just make out across the valley, a world ruled over by evil spirits and buried beneath a melancholy sea of trees. Great camphor trees towered up there, trees with enormous trunks smothered in ivy, and eerie dark shrubberies below. Some gravestones were grimy with moss, the surrounding railings dull gray and rusting, while the clipped hedges and bushes exuded a depressingly damp and stagnant air, and between them ran a maze of black dirt and gravel paths.

One part of the cemetery near the field was particularly uncared for, with a rotting wooden fence crumbling to the ground. On the narrow path of soft black earth in which footprints were easily made one saw the occasional molehill, and the graves there were mostly wretched-looking things. There were a few oddly bright and cheerful ones, and even some that were solemnly imposing, but to neither category belonged two quite unremarkable small graves, and in them slept the brother and sister I had never known.

When our old nanny pointed to one of them and said that was my brother's grave, I would ritually point to the other and say that was my sister's, feeling this was a duty I was obliged to perform. Never having seen them in the flesh, I was quite incapable of comprehending the fact that these two were my brother and sister in just the same way as my living sister was, and I would gaze at the map-like patterns the liverwort had formed on the dark earth, or feel the slippery smooth bark of a tree next to the two graves, and look bored, while Nanny would mumble to herself about all the children in our house being so weak, admonishing me that I at least must grow up into a splendid young man.

If Nanny caught my eye while she was saying this, I merely felt embarrassed, but when my sister was there and had the same thing said to her she would meekly nod her head in agreement. I just couldn't understand what death might be, and the thought that I myself could die and be transformed into stone like this was even more incredible, so it was only natural that I should look bored by it all.

There was one occasion, however, when I thought I had seen the real shape of death. I was standing at the fence while Nanny was kneeling by the graves pulling up weeds, as the blur of dusk drifted over everything, and I was gazing emptily at the nearby trees, when something like a puff of mist slipped up the trunk of one of them and hid itself among the branches. That at least is what I seemed to see; it may well have been some stray shred of mist or merely an illusion, I don't know, but for a moment I felt that death had revealed its power, the extent of its dominion. I blinked my eyes and thought I ought to tell Nanny about it, but she was squatting with her back toward me, and she too looked vague and wavering in that light, which I assumed was also somehow part of the workings of death. So finally I said nothing, feeling only a sudden weariness, and thus death passed me by and vanished somewhere, leaving a certain fear behind, a certain curiosity.

Then one day much later I was walking with my cousin in the cemetery, going nowhere in particular. He was very grown up for his age, and always behaved as if he felt he was too old for me, sneering at me because I sometimes spoke in a way inappropriate for a boy, a habit I suppose I'd picked up from always playing with my sister. Perhaps I was hoping to impress him with my superior knowledge of the cemetery, as I was walking quickly in front of him. I would point out any rounded gravestone made of concrete we came to, and tell him that it belonged to a foreigner. In return, he would stop at any large tomb and pretend he was reading whatever was written on it, since he was already going to school. Unfortunately, although I was still too young for school, I could read quite well, and was sometimes able to work out that he was making it all up. It wasn't that anybody was teaching me at home, but simply that my interest in shapes meant that I started to memorize characters early on in life. So, knowing somehow that I wasn't fooled, my cousin would run off and start leaping up at the branch of a tree and snatching off its leaves, making me try to do this too because I was absolutely hopeless at it.

As evening began to fall I suddenly grew excited and, as though it were something of enormous importance I had forgotten, said I would show him the graves of my brother and sister; but when I looked about me I realized that we had come to a part of the cemetery I'd never been to before, and I had no idea where I was, each path and every gravestone being unfamiliar. The light of the sunset sky seen through the foliage was fading, and one tree ahead of me with grotesquely gnarled branches looked as if it might be swarming with demons. Around the tree was a group of gravestones jostling together, and they had all turned their cold faces in this direction to see what I was up to, seeming to bar my way. Perhaps a little of the panic and confusion I was feeling showed on my face, as my cousin took me by the hand and said we would visit the graves some other day—the best thing now would be to go straight home.

Completely crestfallen, I let him hold my hand and lead me along, like an infant who had only just learned how to walk and had nothing else to rely on but that hand. Yet if I were to grip it too hard, then he might realize how dependent I'd become, snatch his hand away from mine, and even pretend to run away, so I held it as loosely as I could. But the fact that I hadn't the heart to search the paths and graves to try to find my bearings, and was now entrusting my safety to someone else, only made me feel more cowardly still. Fences, tombs, railings, shrubberies drifted past like shadows, and we seemed doomed to travel through an endless maze.

"Look, there's the field just over there." My cousin's sudden cry cheered me up so much I almost burst out laughing. When I looked around I knew exactly where I was, so the two graves must be quite near, and playfully pulling him by the hand I said we could now go and see them. As if to compensate for all the wretched misgivings I'd felt up to this point I seem to have become ridiculously cheerful.

"Just round this way," I said, in the manly tones I'd carefully learned from him. "Behind that tree over there, that one...."

"What tree? What tree are you talking about?" he asked, interrupting me with some annoyance.

"Just over there. The graves are right behind that one." But in my excitement my voice had somehow lost its masculinity, returning to the girlish inflections picked up from my sister, and since I was afraid he might have noticed and started to despise me again I ran off ahead, only to find my way blocked by a

17

fence. Having no intention of going around it, I began scrambling over, with the result that my short trousers managed to get caught on a stake, which sent me tumbling headfirst down the other side. I was too excited to pay much attention to this disaster, however, promptly picking myself up and stepping around the two graves inside the fence, determined to reach the other more familiar site as soon as possible.

Just as I was about to climb the opposite side of this enclosure, I heard my cousin calling out to me, so far off it sounded like the voice of some insect underground. It surprised me so much that I looked back, one knee against the fence, and as I did so the huge tombstones seemed to be leaning over me, and on both sides tall clusters of wooden grave tablets shut out the rest of the world from view. It was like being enclosed in a secret room in one tiny corner of the earth, and suddenly a mysterious numbness began to spread out from some part of my body, seizing me in a total paralysis, as if my own flesh had melted away and been replaced by some other substance.

Eventually I was able to shake off this feeling, my limbs came slowly back to life, and I got over the fence and made my way between the rows of other gravestones, walking in what seemed to be a very gentle kind of trance, from which I awoke to find that I really must have found the place, for there was the familiar tree with its slippery trunk vague and gray in the dusk.

I heard my cousin's voice again, but this time close to my right. He seemed to have come by some roundabout way. I walked a few paces toward him, and he came right up to me before calling me a fool. His voice was harsh and he was obviously out of breath. He seemed to be genuinely annoyed, so I explained in haste that I had found the graves.

"Who wants to look at boring old graves, anyway?" he said,

yet he followed me along and I triumphantly pointed them out. But it only required a brief look to tell me that these were nothing like our family graves, and I raced to the next one, then the next, but all of them were strangers. I stood still, my neck feeling suddenly stiff as I gazed around me. Night was approaching, descending from the trees, thickening, flowing out across the grass, sliding lazily over the ground. I looked toward my cousin as if appealing for help, but he was a little way off and his face was blurred in the fading light, and I could read no expression there.

"Is this really the place?" he asked in a mysteriously low voice, and I nodded and said it was.

"Were they the two graves we saw just now?"

Again I said they were, but much too quickly this time, almost before his words had faded. I regretted the lie, feeling that I'd done something shameful which I could never take back. I remembered the fact of death; it was a presence to me. My cousin must have moved, for I heard the dull sound of his foot disturbing a pebble....

* * *

At this point I want to describe my experience with the butterfly, which seemed so very mysterious at the time. If you rub, or merely touch, the scales of a butterfly's wings they come off as dust in the hand, and it was this silvery substance which gave the episode its strange intensity. We were staying at a hot spring somewhere in the mountains, and we went to look at the nearby waterfall. Father was there; in my mind's eye I can see his slightly bowed back wearing a dark gray jacket and moving on slowly ahead of me. Mother also appears, wearing a skirt of some kind, though I can't remember what color it was. There in the same scene too are my sister and I, standing quite still together listening to a guide explaining some legend about the waterfall to our parents.

My sister, who seemed to be frightened by the noise of the water, was holding my hand tight in hers. As the water thudded into the basin of the fall, it created a white mist drifting about it, and cold droplets were blown by the wind as far as where we were standing. A dull reverberation seemed to rise out of the rocks at our feet, and the surrounding trees were soaked by the spray that lightly shook at times the delicate, small leaves, and their green watercolors then seemed to melt off the branches and slide down into the mist below.

The guide had a very peculiar voice, sounding as if it had been squeezed out of shape by the water's noise though it still remained quite clear, being heard fitfully whenever the thunder of the fall slackened for a moment. I was so interested that I strained to hear it, seeming as it did at times borne in on the cold air, and at others springing out from the shadowy ferns or even from the damp, smooth rocks we were standing on, although whenever I looked at him the sounds were obviously coming from his mouth since it kept opening and shutting. Despite this, I slipped my hand quietly from my sister's, because my neck and arms were freezing in the air rising from the fall, and walked away over the slippery rocks; but she didn't seem to notice and went on standing there alone, looking over at the guide or up at my mother, with a very serious expression on her face.

I came to the back of a teahouse only a little way from the fall. The river valley from that point upstream was used for cultivating horseradish, and the whole area was covered with these plants, although I had no idea at that time what they were. I held on to a wire fence and looked down at the river. The cold air from the waterfall didn't rise this far. Then I suddenly looked up. There was a large tree directly behind me, and the branches came right down to the level of my head. I went on looking upward for a while, entranced by the patterns of sunlight as it filtered between the leaves, seeing them as signs not fully understood, a form of revelation; and in the very next moment that revelation did indeed take place, as from out of a dense, dark patch of foliage a small, dazzlingly bright object fluttered before my eyes.

For a moment I didn't know what it was, aware only of a tingling numbness passing along my spine. A shiver, colder even than the spray of the waterfall, pierced deep inside me. This wasn't a feeling of fear, nor one of joy, but something surpassing either: an experience of intense, pure vision. My whole body rigid, with complete, unwavering attention, I focused on that object suddenly revealed, silvery white and flitting airily about. It was only a small butterfly, and once I realized that, the whole experience should have come to nothing, and yet it still held me spellbound, the movement of its wings too fast to make out as it came and went, a single blur of silver white.

It seemed that the butterfly wanted to settle, so I stuck my arm straight out in front of me, praying that it would land there; and lo and behold it did, softly folding its wings as it rested on the inside of my upper arm. With the tips touching precisely above it and its thin feelers extended, it began to walk slowly along my arm. The tickling sensation this produced was intense, and I could barely stop myself trembling, so I quietly cupped my right hand, then suddenly brought it down over those glistening wings. I don't think this was due merely to a child's possessiveness, but probably more to a desire to put an end to a feeling of suspense that had become unbearable. I could now sense the hopeless fluttering of its wings against my fingers, a peculiarly cheerless sensation, for it seemed to tell me how far I still was from having really caught this mysterious butterfly. In my excitement my grip became too tight, half killing it, and, as if in its last throes, it half opened all four wings there on the palm of my hand. But now the surface of its wings was red, a faded though still lustrous, almost orange shade, darkening toward the edges; yet this was the same butterfly that had been dancing about me, had settled on my arm, and never in that time had it revealed a single trace of red. It was a complete mystery, an example of the same magic my mother had used to make the face disappear from the pattern on the carpet.

I gazed intently at the butterfly in the palm of my hand. The undersides of the wings were definitely silver. Then I noticed that bits of glittering dust had rubbed off on my fingers. I must have been preoccupied by this, and my hand perhaps shook or a sudden breeze came up from the river, for the dead butterfly fluttered upward, spiraling over the wire fence and falling into the valley with its planted rows of horseradish. I looked eagerly for it, but to no avail: the wide expanse of foliage had instantly swallowed up that brilliant speck of light. I gaped down foolishly for a while, then looked at my fingers again. What remained of the dust was so shiny it made me feel uneasy. Nervously I rubbed it all off on the grass at my feet, despite the fact that I regretted doing so as soon as I'd begun.

The place we were staying at was on a cliff above the swift-flowing river. When dinner was over and it had grown dark outside, the noise of the water coming up to us through the trees seemed even louder. I gripped the rail of the little wooden veranda of our room, and looked at other lights which could be seen through the trees, fascinated by their flickering as if it were in some way connected with the roaring that came from the valley. Behind me I heard Mother's voice.

"Do you still remember? Then tell us if you do."

She was trying to get my sister to recite what she'd heard that day about the legend of the waterfall, but the girl was apparently overcome by shyness, standing by my mother's chair and just wriggling from side to side.

"Well, once there was a ... a ..."

"A woodcutter," said Mother helpfully.

"There was a woodcutter. And then he got his foot caught in a spider's web. And the spider was a something sort of spider. What kind of spider was it, now?"

"A harlot spider."

"This spider was living at the bottom of the waterfall...."

With a certain amount of assistance my sister went on with the story, her eyes staring resolutely upward, and swinging her arms about as she did so. She gave her version of it in a long monotone oddly reminiscent of the way the guide had spoken earlier in the day. Her delivery, echoing that other more mysterious voice, which must have made a strong impression on me, seems to have brought a clear recollection of the tale to the surface of my mind; otherwise, I can't explain how I, in spite of being much more naïve than my sister, should have been able to grasp the outline of the legend far more accurately than she did, no matter how vague my understanding of it might have been.

With his dying words the woodcutter had warned his son never to go near the basin of the waterfall, but one day, when the boy had grown up, he accidentally dropped his axe into the waterfall. So the young man disobeyed his father's warning and climbed down the cliff to the basin, and there before a cave at

23

water level he saw a woman spinning. She was a water sprite, the spirit of the place, and, alas—now that he had seen her—his body, along with his axe, was finally found washed up on the bank of the river downstream.

"Was this spider fairy pretty?" asked my sister.

"Yes, she was very pretty indeed," Mother replied, and I thought about the spider woman and what she must have looked like, imagining every possible form I could think of.

The bedding was at last laid out and a big white mosquito net put up. Being inside it felt quite different from the dark green one at home, so we two children romped about for a while, but finally my sister lay down with her arms clasped around her pillow. She always slept on her side, going off to sleep immediately, just like my mother. Only Father lay awake with the bedside lamp still on, reading. I couldn't get to sleep at all, and just lay there looking at the white net and feeling gloomily left out of things. From time to time, attracted by the light, insects came to the window facing the river which had been left open, probably moths of some kind which clung to the net beating their wings, although it was impossible to make out from inside it what color they were. So I began regretfully to recall the silver glitter of that butterfly today. If only the butterfly would come, I thought, looking repeatedly at my fingers, which had once held the mystic shape so firmly in their grasp.

On the verge of sleep, I saw the spirit of the waterfall. She was crouching in the flickering half-light, the very feminine shape I had imagined. She wore a dazzling cloak of some thin material, silver white. Being a sprite, her face of course was not only beautiful but frightening as well, having also something about it reminiscent of my mother. When the specter began to fade, growing small and distant, it seemed more like my sister.

24

As always, I woke up a number of times during the night, and each time my eyes opened, Father's light was still on. Though only half awake, I could even hear the sound as he turned over a page, while to my blurred vision the white, hanging folds of the mosquito net gave the impression of being at the bottom of the sea, which was somehow satisfying. A number of moths were still clinging to the netting, their wings unmoving now, but it seemed that no silver-white butterfly had appeared....

That vague impression of my father was my last of him. He died somewhere up north, in a remote river town, once a thriving port but nothing now. According to a pamphlet about him which a student of his compiled, Father had suffered from angina pectoris for years, and it was a heart attack from which he'd died. Despite the constant suffering life had imposed on him, he appears to have felt a deep if unspoken affection for this world up until the end.

For a short time the house was full of bustle and noise, a noise made all the more prominent by the silence that the dark, dank rooms had maintained till then. It was as if the house were doing this on purpose, the various objects in that silence—the stairs, the narrow passageway, the stacks of books, the dust long undisturbed in various corners—emptily proclaiming that such peace and quiet could never be obtained elsewhere.

I mourned, subdued and dull, amid the crowd of books. A weak sunlight came through the window, faintly illuminating the leather covers of the ones piled on the floor, emphasizing the finger marks made in the dust. The countless books preserved their usual silence, and I stood among them, gazing about me with straining eyes, thinking that perhaps the impossible might happen and now I would be shown the proper face of death. I was breathing heavily through my nose, and I became aware of a particular odor, though "stench" might be a better word. I have a very clear recollection of this, it being a smell so well defined I could never confuse it with the various odors I'd encountered in the field outside. Certainly it was the dank smell of the ancient room, the books, the dust, the mildew, all of these; but it also included the smell of my father, for the odor his body gave off was of a very special kind. I experienced this most in the vicinity of his desk, where, in retrospect, the smell of books predominated.

Still, I was sure I'd recognized the odor of my father, of his actual presence, and at that moment I felt arise in me an overwhelming sense of his closeness, of being near him and at peace. I knew that he had been taken away from us by death while on a journey. I knew there was no longer any question of his being anywhere. And yet I sensed him about me in this lingering smell, and now I was standing in the place where he used to be. It may have been wishful thinking, but this gave me the conviction somehow that Father and I were one, were sharing the same existence.

For the first time in my life I took down one of the books from the shelves, having always felt till then that they were things to be kept at a respectful distance. The book was a hardcover volume of paintings, so large I was only just able to hold it in my hands. The pages had become stuck together with the humidity, and as I turned them they made a slight crackling sound, and that same smell seemed to emanate anew from the thick, blotched paper. Unconsciously I was imitating my father, back slightly bowed, head cocked a little to the left, with a childishly incompetent show of irritation, too. I looked at gloomy landscapes with various people dressed in medieval costume. One elaborate illustration of the intricacies of a battlefield particularly intrigued me, as I tried painstakingly to work out which were people and which were horses. It was much like my earlier efforts to interpret the pattern in my mother's carpet, and I remained absorbed in it for some time; but finally I closed the book and gazed up at the dark, stained ceiling, reflecting that when I grew up I would have this room and my sister would have Mother's; a reflection which made me feel strangely depressed, as if some sudden silence had occupied my mind.

Far from suffering a decline, however, the attraction of my mother's room seemed even stronger than before. Only, from that point on I found the large mirror no longer pleased me, for it was now merely an object that reflected the mahogany dressing table, Mother's beautiful clothes, Mother herself, and my sister's pretty face; and when it also reflected the occasional house guest, it seemed to be reminding me how irrelevant my own presence was, how inferior I was to the kind of person this room accepted.

Once when I wandered in there for no reason, I was brought up short by the appearance in the mirror of an image I had never seen before. It was only my mother, but she was almost naked to the waist, something her children were never allowed to see; or at least I had no recollection of it, for I was brought up on cow's milk, not my mother's, and the concept of a woman's breast was almost a complete blank to me. Our old nanny had sometimes let me touch her withered dugs when I slept with her as a small child, but I hadn't felt the slightest interest. Yet Mother's body was quite dazzlingly white, and the sight of those soft, round swellings was attractive to me; and her loosened hair, tinged with brown, fell in languid waves over her shoulders.

As was my habit with any new sight, I decided to fix it firmly in my mind, exactly as I did when discovering some rare species of flora or fauna.

* * *

After my father died, she was often away for days at a time. We children tried to hide our unhappiness from each other by getting up to various kinds of mischief, such as taking the bottles out of the drinks cupboard in the parlor and playing at entertaining guests. On these occasions I did my level best to copy my cousin's breezy manner, pouring some amber-colored liquid into a glass and gallantly offering it to my sister as if it were something I did almost every day. This she usually declined with a modest shake of the head, but once she wickedly decided to try some, pulling a hideous face at the first small sip of it. It seemed only right that I should join her, so I took hold of a bottle of wine the color of blood, removed the long cork shaped like the neck of a clown, and poured some into another glass. I then swallowed it, screwing up my face as though drinking poison, which so amused my sister that she produced a deep, delighted gurgle in her throat, while I proceeded to lurch and totter about, pretending to be tipsy. But I tottered so much that eventually I realized I was genuinely drunk, only just avoiding going flat on my face when I stumbled, and realizing too that my eyes seemed somehow to be melting. I felt inordinately sluggish all over, although there was nothing in the least unpleasant about the feeling, probably because I was free at last for a while from the usual niggling anxieties that filled my days.

At night we used to sleep in the room next to the hall. It was quite ordinary in size but looked enormous when the bedding had been put down, and we always slept a little apart from each

28

other. As soon as the light was switched off, my sister closed her eyes, yielding at once to sleep, the imitation death that summoned her each night. But I just lay there open-eyed, hoping to grow accustomed to the dark—no imitation, but an actual presence. If I kept my eyes open, the darkness would flow steadily into them, filtering through and eventually occupying all my body; and once that had happened I would have nothing more to fear, for the night and I were now as one and I could go off to sleep with only my mouth wide open.

One evening in winter (it must have been winter because it was cold), sometime after midnight, I think, I suddenly woke up and, still partly immersed in the world of dreams, found myself listening to some sound I couldn't yet identify. It turned out to be voices coming from the hall, and soon afterward I was aware of Nanny going past our door. My sister suddenly jumped out of bed so I tried to follow suit, but I felt as if I might immediately collapse, for my feet seemed to be treading on clouds. My whole body was overwhelmed with tiredness, and I wasn't sure if I was dreaming or not, but we held each other's hands, shivering in the cold, and made our way toward the dim light that filtered from the hall.

"It's Mummy," cried my sister when we saw her standing there, and I did the same, feeling strange that words should issue from my mouth. Mother said something to Nanny who went to take her coat, but Mother kept it on, saying something else to her again. Nanny then went away. I felt annoyed at not being able to follow any of this properly. Then Mother looked at us for the first time and put her hands very gently on our heads.

"You'll catch cold, so go back to bed."

At least that's what I think she said. For some reason, I got excited and took hold of her hand with both of mine. It was as

29

cold as ice, so cold I didn't know what to do, wondering if I should try to warm it in mine or just let it go; and again the desire to sleep came over me, and all my surroundings seemed to grow dark, when suddenly we were caught up in her arms. So fierce was the embrace I could hardly breathe—I thought I'd faint—and somewhere in my chest I felt that deep exhaustion which, even now, I always feel in times of stress.

When Mother finally released us and made her way upstairs, it was as if some secret understanding had been reached between us, for we stood dutifully at the bottom of the stairs and watched her go. At some point, we had joined hands again.

Once she had gone into her room we two went back to bed, but I felt a peculiar fluttering about my heart, whether of fear or joy or both I didn't know, and was quite unable to sleep. Finally I started to giggle, and heard an answering giggle from my sister's bed. This made me laugh more and more, until my sister sat up and, in a voice which she only just managed to keep from trembling with laughter herself, told me sharply to stop it. I told her not to be so cheeky, and reached out to thump her bedclothes, but we were too far apart and my hand only slapped the cold floor between us. Even so this made her shout out, almost scream, that she would tell Mother, but I refused to give in and said I would tell her too, so we both got up and went out into the hallway.

In the room under the staircase a light still glowed, and we stood at the bottom of the stairs and scowled at each other, until she looked up at the floor above and said "Mummy" in a tiny voice. The sound was immediately swallowed up in the darkness drifting down the stairs, so this time I called out, but in a voice as faint as possible, virtually a whisper.

The silence upstairs remained undisturbed. We looked at each other and laughed for no reason, her voice sounding as if she had something ticklish deep in her throat. We were still dressed only in our pyjamas and were getting cold. No longer having any inclination to quarrel, we drew close together and called out in one voice:

"Mummy."

We must have made a charming picture, like two kittens huddled together, but there was still no response from above so we shouted out again, in voices now full of anxiety and dismay.

Mother appeared this time, soundlessly, suddenly, moving very slowly and calmly as if she had understood everything, raising her right hand as if to restrain us, her thrust-out fingers oddly like those of someone swimming through the dark. Her whole appearance was blurred and white, no doubt because she was wearing her white dressing gown; and yet what always surprises me about this memory of her is how sharp its details seem now, how clear. Despite the almost total darkness at the top of the stairs, I can still remember the expression on her face, the loosened hair drifting in soft waves behind her shoulders, and the intense, black eyes as they looked down on us. A slight, sad smile appeared on her lips, and she moved her outstretched hand up and down, twice, three times, a gesture that suggested a hidden distress; then she opened her mouth and said something, although what it was I couldn't hear. To me it was like watching a film when the sound breaks down and the actors are made suddenly dumb, moving their lips but only miming speech, and at once I felt afraid; but it was also as if I had lost all willpower and could only go on standing there looking up at her, beautiful but indistinctly so, like an image formed in a feverish, semiconscious mind.

Probably my sister heard what she had said, for timidly she took my hand and said we should go back to bed; and on hearing her voice I at last realized that I was freezing cold. So we fled back to our beds, curling up again in their friendly warmth, although I imagined Mother still standing there, lingering there a long time, calm and at rest. And, strangely, sleep came over me quite soon, like a slow wave breaking, holding me in its long, complete embrace. I still don't understand how I was able to fall asleep so quickly and so peacefully.

When I woke up next morning Mother had gone. Nanny said she had gone away on a journey again. But she never came back.

We pretended we knew all about what had happened that night, so we asked the grown-ups nothing, only talking occasionally to each other; and whenever we did this we would make a point of giggling, or look at each other with absurdly rounded eyes, mimicking a shocked distress we thought we didn't feel. Once my sister used the words "Mummy's ghost," but I was so shaken by what seemed to me the unforgivable that strong disapproval must have shown in the expression on my face, for she never used such words again.

Eventually we were taken to live with our uncle, who was Father's elder brother. Quite soon after that, however, my sister found a home elsewhere, though not among the living but the dead.

The natural world surrounding me, the new life in everything I saw, the scent of foliage and of the earth, the sense of light, all this was almost unintelligible. On the borders of the road, which was gradually getting steeper now, the fresh, abundant leaves were starting to change in color slightly, and swarms of bees and gadflies were choking themselves on the rich pollen from the shrubberies in bloom. In places, brushwood had been spilled by the side of the road, where patches of heat rippled and dissolved, but in the shadows one could feel the cool, even cold air of the mountains. Yet at this same point in time the war, though now approaching its end, was still raging on, and the Tokyo I'd left just a few days before, like numerous other places in Japan, was probably engulfed in the roar of exploding bombs, the rattle of the guns replying. Even here in the mountains of Shinshū, about a hundred miles northwest of Tokyo, a squadron of B-29s had passed overhead last night, on their way to drop mines in the port of Niigata. But here everything throbbed with reborn life, and it was this that seemed so mysterious—the fact that, quite unrelated to that other world, this natural one should go on radiantly living.

When people in fairy tales finally awaken from a deep, enchanted sleep, they must find themselves in a similar predicament, wondering if all they've seen in their fragmented dreams isn't ultimately real, and this fresh, much clearer-looking world merely an illusion. And, with my boyhood now drawing to a close, I shared their sense of dislocation as I walked along.

It may be a mistake to consider childhood as a form of slumber, a period when the spiritual life is at rest, yet it does seem that, in order to allow the harvest sown in infancy to ripen, some form of sleep, some unawareness of the dull stereotypes surrounding us, is called for. In my case there was also the war which, as has often been said, was like an endless holiday, providing an excessively long period of inactivity for those who hadn't come of age. So it was not surprising that a boy of that time, brought up in this vacuum, should have grown only in the sense of physical height and the accumulation of years, becoming virtually indistinguishable from other people of the same age.

Around me the trunks of the larches went on patiently growing, and from the stumps of those recently cut down arose the smell of sawdust. In the delicate, bluish light filtering through the pine needles, small butterflies, probably some kind of skipper, fluttered about, looking as if their slender, deep brown wings had been made on purpose to absorb the rays of passing sunlight, while the light itself seemed to pour down only in order to play with the quiet shadows of the powdery wings. On the oily leaves of the bushes the sawfly larvae lay neatly curled, and there were also weevils stretching out their weird, long necks, and small beetles with shiny backs like precious stones, dragging soft leaves to serve as cradles for their young. All this activity, the unsullied light, and a quiet which invaded one's whole body worked their influence on me, bringing me to life.

It was June of the final year of the Pacific War. I was eighteen, and I had passed the entrance exam for a high school in this region, but since the war situation had become so critical, admission was indefinitely postponed, and I'd been obliged to remain a middle-school student drafted into munitions work. The reason I'd been able to leave Tokyo just a few days before was that in the air raid at the end of May both my uncle's house where I lived and the factory in which I'd been working had been burned to the ground. I had only to move back about a fortnight in time to be confronted by the stench of benzine, the blinding sparks flying from the bite of the finishing tool, the spirals of steel shavings, the rows of houses torn down to make firebreaks, the wail of the sirens, white vapor trails high up in the sky, tracer shells lighting up the night, and huge conflagrations that reduced everything to ashes. Not that this led to any sense of horrifying confusion, for it was, on the contrary, a thoroughly methodical destruction. What could have been more orderly in the searchlight beams than a formation of those monstrous duralumin birds, what more polished and refined, what more calculated to inspire one's admiration?

By contrast, now it was a leaf, a clod of earth, a ray of sunlight that caught my eye; and yet the sense of the particular, of the individual object or event, was absent in these plain, calm, indifferent things, belonging more to the world I'd left behind than

35

here. What they expressed was a much more fundamental concept of the type, the species, that basic idea which dominates nature, that of the object repeating itself, and it was this underlying purpose which had such power to move the heart, to cause it pain and arouse whatever lay sleeping there.

Worn out by hunger and the unfamiliar terrain, I sat down on a pile of brushwood by the side of the road. I had only eaten a bit of rice and vegetables that morning, and seemed to have no energy from the waist down at all. So I sat there, looking at a silver birch, its pale trunk with the bark peeling slightly, its bunches of leaves swaying in the light breeze, and felt only the faintest sensation of time passing. In the city I had just left, a place of blackened emptiness and rubble, time rushed forward from one violent moment to the next. But here its process seemed almost circular, as if the moments hesitated in their going, toying with the present.

While I went on resting, I gazed at the endless clarity of the sky, the small birds hopping about from branch to branch. In the rustling of the leaves I heard an invitation to set off again, though I was listening to another sound as well perhaps, of something falling far off in the woods. Many odors mingled in the sunlight, including the smell of my own sweat, and as I still sat there idly dangling my tired legs, I was equally aware of both the inviting murmurs of the world about me and the exhaustion of my body. For a long time I had forgotten what it was like to be able to give in to the demands of a tired body.

Just then, a gadfly settled on my chest, and when I casually brushed it off a sudden, weird idea took hold of me: what if this hand of mine were paralyzed, incapable of movement? The thought was so unexpected that I looked down at my chest. Obviously the hand went on moving and the insect flew away, but it seemed like someone else's hand, moving of its own accord. For some reason, I then felt a great wave of affection pass through me, a surge of feeling for something long held dear, though what it was I couldn't tell. The wave broke and fell away. Time must have been playing some game with me, perhaps, and now the wave had receded, slipped back again to curl among the branches of the silver birches as if nothing strange had happened.

Someone called out to me and I opened my eyes. It was a man in his late fifties with a bundle of firewood on his back, obviously a local. He asked me if I was all right, and I told him I was hungry, so he put his hand—its skin looked unusually thick—into the pouch at his waist and pulled out a reddish brown object which he then gave me. It was a sort of bread, made out of millet and crumbled into pieces. I stuffed it into my mouth so quickly I could hardly breathe for a moment. He told me it would take about two hours of steady walking to reach the top. He also said he had to get on, and get on he did, moving slowly up the road, now only a path, with his load wobbling on his back. I bowed my head after him, and watched for a while as he deliberately moved one leg forward then the other, and it was perhaps to the same rhythm as his measured pace that I felt I was making my own journey into the past.

After a while I rediscovered the energy to walk, stood on my own two feet again, and started plodding up the mountain path, which suddenly got steep and began to zigzag. I was soon panting and gasping for breath, but my legs went on bearing me along, and my mind seemed to become even more detached and at peace as I thought about a number of things. My eyes, however, still took in the scenery around me, recording how the face of nature was changing, while the path I was climbing became more stony and occasional bushes blocked my passage. I also came across a number of large anthills, belonging to a species of ant known both for the sharp smell of formic acid it gives off and for its persistent habit of crawling up one's legs; and I noticed that my hand, of its own accord again, was either brushing them off or holding one out occasionally for my inspection.

At last I arrived at the peak, an outcrop of black earth among the surrounding rocks. A raised platform had been built in the center, made of slate-like stones simply piled one on the other, and a row of stone Buddhas had been placed there. The gently rippling tableland of Utsukushigahara stretched away, and looking back in the direction from which I'd come I saw the enormous waves of the Northern Alps, encircling the plain of Matsumoto near at hand and then extending far into the distance. I was tired out by the climb but not to the point of real exhaustion, so I sat down with the platform of stone images at my back and gazed at the whole scene that was offered me: at the plain stretched out peacefully with its rivers' veins, at the mountain shapes beyond, the great unending wall adorned with last year's snow in places, fading into the dark blue of the distance where the various peaks of the far Alps lay in all their massiveness and weight, the delicate interplay of shadows and the rows of crests rising together into the sky.

The sky was so transparently clear it had achieved a certain darkness, as if that endless distance had cast a kind of shadow. Where the blue depths descended on the farthest mountains it made them shine a perfect white, a full circle on the horizon of total purity, of a pure, unfeeling cold. This was an absolute silence, filling everywhere, and in the midst of it I sat, motionless, thinking of nothing, not even trying to think.

With my legs stretched out before me I went on sitting there for a long time, doing nothing but breathe lightly, and all I heard was something that was no sound but only an obscure sense of distance and space transmitted to me from the mountain range. Then in the silence the sound of my breath and this soundless calling from the mountains seemed to be hovering in the space about me, to be whisperingly gathering near. Finally a word emerged from that emptiness, a word my own lips then shaped in response, a completely unlooked-for word, one which at first I didn't recognize and which my lips had to form once more before I understood; and when I had done so and tasted its full meaning I felt only a confused sense of its irrelevance. Why should a word I hadn't used for so many years, the childish word I had used to call out to my mother and now long forgotten, why should it make an abrupt reappearance at a time like this? Could it be that it had taken such deep root inside me that it needed this unique sense of desolation, of an immense void, to draw it out again? I had no close relatives, and for some time I had been separated from those with whom I'd spent the major part of my life, so a mere sense of loneliness, of being an isolated speck of life on this bleak mountaintop, would not in itself have been enough; nor would the knowledge that by tomorrow I would be involved again somewhere in the war. And yet, surrounded as I was by the unfailing presence of the natural world, I found the word I muttered—"Mummy"—provoked an urgent question, which, for all its banality, is one we never tire of asking: where had I really come from?

In an effort to reply, I searched my memory, trying my hardest to revive the vague and fading past. There were scenes I could remember clearly enough, such as my first day at school, when I underwent a simple medical test, had a green ribbon stuck on my chest to indicate the class I was in, and then walked along a creaking corridor crying because I couldn't find the class-room; but the film sequence broke off at that point, as happened with all such recollections, where pitch-darkness always closed in around the thin, wavering light of whatever path I might be fol-lowing. I suppose anyone's memories of their infancy are bound to be fairly hazy, in places no more than fragments of the past, but in my case all that had happened to me before I went to live with my uncle was a total blank, as if the gradually narrowing road back into the past suddenly ended at the edge of a great cliff. Certainly I knew, at least to some extent, about my father, mother, and sister and the house we used to live in; but this was all purely abstract information with not one shred of lived expe-rience among it. I could just about remember my sister's death, but not one single image, not even the most perfunctory, re-mained of my parents. I had learned about my father at my uncle's place, and could faintly recall photos of him I'd been shown in the family album; but of my mother there had been nothing, for there seemed to be some secret connected with the nature of her disappearance, and the adults maintained a strict si-lence about it. It is quite possible that I myself had always been unconsciously avoiding the issue as well; and yet somehow I had acquired the knowledge that Mother had died at some time or other. When exactly I had learned this wasn't clear at all, as the information must have been just passively acquired, and yet it seemed positive for all that; for the certainty of it, like many other facts of the same concealed kind, I could feel permeating my skin like a sort of warmth. But this still didn't mean that all my earliest memories, and thus my whole infancy itself, were not completely lost. For no reason I could understand, I had felt sud-denly compelled to inquire into my past, in particular to seek some appearance of my mother there, and yet not one image had presented itself to me. A few pieces of information, some mere abstractions I could find; but even these were more like fairy tales told long ago, as relevant to me now as the pictures in a storybook I could remember seeing at some far-off point in time on a bookstall somewhere.

A sudden fear came over me, an apprehension that what my existence had been based upon was canceled at one stroke, that I had been reduced to the ambiguity of a shadow; and I shook my head as if to rid myself of it. There was a singing sound deep in my ears, but I was unable to make out if this was a result of my anxiety or only the sound I thought I had been hearing up till then from the distant range of mountains. Those mountains alone remained unchanged, magnificent in their linked immensity, but the very sense of distance, of apartness they evoked only made me more despondent still. Finally I stood up and, looking at the huge spearhead of Mt. Yarigadake, I muttered to myself a peculiarly stupid thought which occurred to me then, wondering whether that peak would remain unscathed if a sixteen-inch shell smashed into it.

Thus my infancy had disappeared, and no doubt the process whereby it was lost had been a simple one of mere forgetting. And yet, just as a child is not a small version of an adult, so an infant is not merely a small child, although what mysterious laws control these differences is a question I should probably leave to others. Perhaps all one can say is that the aim of infancy, only the aim, is simply that of growth, of arriving at the next stage of development, and this is why anything that hinders the process, be it an experience or a memory of one, is just hidden quietly away within the personality somewhere, in the same way that tuberculosis bacilli are hemmed in by a calcified wall which they themselves have secreted. But this also means that each of us

41

must carry an unknown burden on his back, the dark world of the unconscious, a shadow which remains until our death, growing larger with the years.

If this is so, then there was nothing strange about the absolute lack of recall I experienced on that mountain. It merely meant that one stage of life had been accomplished; the process was achieved, complete. If the illness I suffered later on in childhood had not occurred, and if a strange excavation of the heart had never taken place, then no doubt I would have come to believe that I had been born at my uncle's house, that this was where I'd really come from. And thus I would have spent a lifetime never understanding why those heavy gravestones, those mysterious patterns on a carpet, appeared so often in my dreams. But for the moment let us leave all that, and consider instead some aspects of my boyhood, the earliest moments of my life that memory at that time was able to reach.

* * *

Great Uncle, as Nanny called my uncle, ran a fairly big private hospital in the suburbs of Tokyo. His family consisted almost entirely of doctors, and only fifty yards or so from his house were the two buildings that made up the hospital he'd built himself. This vision of the hospital as an extension of the extended family had started with my grandfather, who had two of his three sons become doctors and conscientiously married off both daughters to doctors as well, the only exception being made in the case of my father.

The enormous, decaying house, a monument to a more spacious age, was occupied by over twenty people, not counting the various employees, although it was well nigh impossible to work out precisely who was related in what way to whom. The place had almost nothing in common with the concept of the home that people nowadays seem to have, being no unit but a conglomeration of individuals who looked after their own bits of territory and whose attitude toward each other was an odd mixture of intimacy and plain indifference. The building itself reflected this social pattern, for extra bits were always being tacked on here and there, awkwardly connected by various passageways, so that someone visiting for the first time could easily find himself unable to make his way outside again. One would come across a really dilapidated, mildewed room on the verge, it seemed, of immediate collapse, and yet right next door to it would be a living room neat and sparkling with its brand-new wood. If one then assumed this was the direction things were going in, there next appeared a smart Western-style room, in the most refined architectural taste, containing a cheap, battered piano in a corner with most of the varnish peeling off it. It was also quite easy for somebody to become ill in this house and nobody know anything about it until he was better again. This indifference was common, and any minor alterations in almost any aspect of life that occurred there were treated with a complete lack of interest.

Consequently, when my sister and I were swallowed up into this environment it hardly created a ripple. The grown-ups did not concern themselves with us newly arrived children in the various ways one might have expected, but neither did they treat us coldly; they just let us be. The relationships even between parent and child in this house, though frank and open, involved an indefinable sense of distance, and so our position didn't seem in the least unusual. Obviously, growing up in these surroundings meant that I acquired various emotional and mental attitudes conditioned by them; but that, of course, is what this story is all about.

My sister died soon after we arrived. I'm not sure if I have already made this clear, but she was an exceptionally beautiful and charming child. There are certain people who seem to have been born to die rather than to live, and these people singled out by death are remarkably gentle, made in a particularly sensitive mold, as if death were thus proclaiming its superiority to life. My sister was one of these special people. Later on, whenever the grown-ups decided to make some comment on the oddness of my features, they would inevitably draw a comparison with hers.

"Your sister was such a lovely little girl," my grandmother would say, in that rather distant tone of voice which seems a characteristic of old age. "I can't think why you should have turned out looking like a flying squirrel."

My grandmother made a habit of using these animal analogies, and each time she said something nasty she would think of a different one. For this reason, I was compared to a frog, an ostrich—all sorts of things—but I knew I had no right to complain because my sister really had been very beautiful: slim, extremely fragile, a creation made with meticulous care, like a handicraft doll. That death should have taken her away so suddenly when she was still a little girl must mean that death had doted on her, stroking her with its cold, funereal hands and ensuring that nothing spoiled the perfection of her looks. There had also been something almost courtly in the form of its invitation to its realm, a calm submission in the manner of her going.

One morning, when everybody was bustling about as usual, she suddenly collapsed and became incapable of speech. The grown-ups said it was dysentery, but I assume that death had already come to receive her as its own, sitting by her side and watching over her with solemn, even slightly unhappy eyes.

They started giving her injections of Ringer's solution. I was sitting in a corner of the room, knees correctly pressed together, watching the activities of the doctor my uncle had called in. From the glass container the transparent liquid passed through a rubber tube, then through a large needle into my sister's thigh, and I watched the whole process with unwavering attention. When the needle had been inserted she had made a very slight grimace, an inquisitive twitching of the cheek, as if she had awoken briefly from a dream but was still only semiconscious. She then opened her lips a fraction, lips now turned purple, and gave a little cry of pain, but that was all. Once the needle had been stuck in she went back to sleep again. Perhaps even the cry of pain was no such thing, but only a light gasp of breath. It takes time for that sort of breath to take the shape of words, and perhaps they had all merely imagined she was complaining that it hurt. To me it had sounded more like a gasp of pleasure, even a voluptuous sigh.

With the injection over, the doctor helped to rearrange the bedclothes, frowned and stroked his cheek pensively. He then had a conversation with my uncle full of portentous-sounding foreign words which I couldn't help finding funny. The eiderdown also happened to be of a particularly garish design, with overblown peonies on it, and this made matters worse. Knowing I would be scolded if I laughed, I slipped quietly out of the room.

It was now well into the rainy season, with low gray clouds covering the sky; one of those days when if only a slight break were to appear in the clouds and a strip of blue show through, summer would have begun. But of this there was no sign, so it was just another day in the most oppressive and melancholy of seasons. I looked out into the garden, and around the huge old dogwood tree near the fence a whitish swarm of moths was dancing about, looking as if a storm of confetti were circling in the air. Every year after that, always in the same season, I would come across similar swarms of these daylight moths, which emerged at this time. Their larvae fed on the leaves of the dogwood, eating every available leaf as though they had some personal grudge against the tree.

One moth lay clinging to the coarse, worn bark of the tree. With white wings half opened, and squirming, jerking movements of the abdomen, it was laying eggs. I approached and observed it closely, noticing how repulsive its face was, the small, blackish brown eyes having already the dull glitter of some inanimate object. I decided it must be going to die. My sister would also be dead quite soon. As I watched the convulsions of the moth I remembered her, and I thought with great earnestness about death. Death must be on very good terms with my mother and sister, as I'd been told that Mother had gone a long, long way away, and I believed that only death could have taken her so far. My father had only been allowed to go after a long and painful struggle, whereas she had been simply called away. It seemed then that death probably wouldn't bother itself with me, and the thought made me unhappy. Nervously I brushed the moth to the ground with my puny hand, then crushed it underfoot. A yellow liquid stained its white belly, now further dirtied by mud. When all trace of the original moth had vanished into pulp at last I felt at ease.

As it happened, my sister died within twelve hours. She died in her sleep, and nobody could tell when the sleep ended and death began. I saw two or three people with eyes swollen from weeping. At first glance it was ugly, but on looking closer I noticed how beautiful their eyes were when wet with tears. I had never seen such softness in them, such gentleness. It astonished me. As I grew older I thought more and more that death must be a very gentle thing.

Once my sister had gone, the enormous house became an empty place for me, an alien, unintelligible environment, just as the huge cemetery had been. The only person who could make me feel at peace with the world was Nanny, who still slept at my side even though I was going to school by then. Sometime in the past she had been in charge of the servants in this house, and she had taken on her present post out of blind love for us, and this passionate concern for the inhabitants of the former house of books was now all concentrated on me alone. It seemed to radiate from every pore of her soft, plump, cheerful, ponderous body, which in its movements was not unlike a very docile Indian elephant.

I often became ill: not only in cold spells but whenever there was some change in the weather I would almost invariably go down with some kind of fever. At such times Nanny would get into a dreadful state, scolding anybody, no matter who it was, who dared walk past my room with heavy steps, and patiently pressing the ice bag down on my burning forehead. She had very little faith in modern medicines, preferring instead her own concoction of muddy-looking hot rice water obtained after hours and hours of boiling. She would top it off with a bright red pickled plum and urge her delirious patient to drink it down. When at last I recovered she was still very reluctant to allow me to get up, insisting that I go on eating rice gruel for a number of days. This gruel was of a very thick consistency, like porridge or mush, and she would wrap small portions of it in leaves of pickled white cabbage and pop them into my mouth, which I would open readily like a baby bird. Each time, Nanny would identify this offering with someone we both knew.

"This one is nice and thin, just like Auntie Chiyo. And here we have a really fat one, like your great uncle."

"No it's not," I'd say. "It's Nanny."

I didn't in fact like going to school that much, but I think probably the main reason I had so many days in bed was because I tended to enjoy being ill. That feverish heaviness of the body, even the spasms of pain, I didn't find all that unpleasant; and there were things I really enjoyed, like the red line zigzagging up and down the thermometer, the pickled plum staining the white gruel a brilliant crimson, the sensation of the ice bag as it seemed to permeate my skin. I suppose this was just one more aspect of my longing for death, which I imagined as a place where an invisible hand would lead me, somewhere at the bottom of the sea where the water lay softly upon the body in perfect peace. I suffered from nightmares at the time, sitting up in the middle of the night and producing some unintelligible grunting sounds, and Nanny would take me in her arms, rocking me gently and stroking my head, telling me that there was nothing there, nothing to harm me. As I gradually calmed down she would usually say:

"You see, it's all the doing of that little insect inside you. Maybe you'd better swallow some insect powder. That'll drive it away, won't it?"

Mostly when I went outside the house it was to a pond near the back garden fence where I used to like to sit quite still with both legs in the water. The water was almost black, and between the lotus leaves floating here and there occasional bubbles of gas would plop up on the surface, discharged from the thick mud at the bottom. I would wiggle my toes about, and through that turbid water they looked like weird little creatures with a life of their own, frolicking together in the depths. In fact when I examined them more closely I began to have serious doubts that these things were actually attached to my own feet, for they seemed to move about, then become still, in a way unrelated to any influence on my part. Sometimes I even felt that my legs, my arms as well, right up to my trunk, had become another species of existence independent of me. This was a state of mind I found I could induce, whenever I felt depressed, by waggling my head about. I would close my eyes, nod my head up and down, and this would act as a form of self-hypnosis. When it went really well I found I was incapable of moving my legs no matter how hard I tried, although as soon as I was convinced of the fact my joints would spring back into action. I also had the ability of seeing at will all sorts of illusions, and when I'd grown tired of this game of dissociation I could still pass the time briefly conjuring up any number of birds and plants.

Yet time passed relentlessly, inevitably, transforming me into a boy of obviously backward tendencies. Just as the mysteries lying hidden in the field of my early childhood had gradually faded, so the inmates of the enormous house ceased to be enigmas and became familiar to my eyes, people I was used to and people I loved. So by degrees I came to forget the past, and at least at the surface level of my memory I lost all trace of my earliest years.

* * *

When exactly this was I am not sure, but it was certainly summer because I remember the sound of the cicadas. I had a peculiar interest in cicadas, particularly the larvae known as nymphs. It was dusk and, as I did every day, I slipped out of the house trembling inside with the secret known to nobody else. There was a wood of oak trees at the back of the house, and that was where I went to collect them. As darkness fell, the low yet piercing stridulation would gradually cease, and when the mosquitoes began swarming above the underbrush the nymphs, which were now turning into adult cicadas, appeared out of the earth.

Although I had double the ordinary share of timidity, the deep attraction of the nymphs canceled out my fears. Straining my eyes in the dark, I looked from one thick tree trunk to another. I discovered a number of their holes in the ground, also some of the shed skins attached to the trunks, but it wasn't so easy to find a nymph that had not yet turned into a cicada. When I did see one, climbing up a tree or just emerging from a hole after its long period underground, and noticed how cautiously it moved, how hesitantly, I felt a sudden tightening about the heart.

After I'd caught one or two of them, and felt the powerful forelegs gripping the palm of my hand, I became aware of my surroundings again, now fully enveloped in the dark from which the shadowy figures of trees appeared threateningly like monsters. Maybugs, awake at last from their daytime sleep, were flying about, sometimes banging into the branches and producing an unnerving clatter with their shards. Through the bushes I could see the lights of the house, and I suddenly panicked and dashed back.

Firmly closing the door of my room (I now slept alone at night), I let the cicada nymphs go. They then clambered up the wooden pillars and window frames, and long after the light was turned off, toward midnight, their backs split open and wonderfully neat-formed young cicadas were born. I struggled to stay awake until this happened, but even if I did drop off to sleep I was in the habit of often waking up anyway, and each time I would cautiously put on the light and see how far they had progressed.

Unless one has actually seen a cicada when it first emerges from its shell it is impossible to imagine the unique attraction of the sight, the soft fragility, as if one touch alone would suffice to disperse this dreamlike image, the tenuous beauty of creatures that could never be born in the light of day. The dark brown cicada has pure white wings when newly born, a moist, lucid, bewitching white. The body also is white, that of some ghostly being from the world of fairy tales. Once it has got the upper half of its body free from its shell it bends over so that it seems to be lying on its back, thus using the weight of its body to extract the rest of itself from the husk. There is an almost heartbreaking artlessness in the movement, as there is, too, in the way it quietly readjusts itself afterward, still clinging on in elegant white nakedness to its discarded self. I would stare wide-eyed at it, forgetting everything in a shared sense of strain, as if my soul were being sucked out of my body.

This exclusive passion for cicada nymphs was gradually transformed into a more general obsession with other sorts of insects. Even the dull horsefly and plain maybug intrigued me, the nervure of the wings and shards revealing a pattern of intricate design. Lying on my back among the grass I would give these insects a very thorough inspection. Some were like velvet to the touch, but with prickly feelers as well, and meaningful-looking configurations on their backs like a secret script, all with a startling luster. Some would leave the dust from their wings on my fingers, others make a cheerful buzzing in my ear, or crawl

51

over the palm of my hand trailing behind a bittersweet smell. I reveled in this form, that color, that touch, never tiring of them.

Above a patch of dry earth between the tussocks of grass large wasps would busily fly back and forth, fluttering their orange wings. This color would change according to the quality of the sunlight, sometimes scarlet, sometimes a burning flame. On the leaves of the bushes there were beetles that shone gold and sapphire, and if you touched them they'd curl up and roll off onto the ground, pretending they were dead. They fell quite naturally, like drops of dew, and it didn't seem to hurt them at all.

A child's obsession with things like brightly colored stones and insects, his desire to possess them, presumably conceals a longing to be like the objects he covets, to become them even. In my case I imagined being a nocturnal moth, the death's-head pattern woven on my wings, flying carelessly in the dark; or a stag beetle, encased in dreadful armor, blithely climbing the rugged oak tree bark. So whenever I found any special insects that really pleased me, I would catch them and put them in a small glass bottle, and even when they were dead and shriveled up I would take them out at times and secretly examine them.

Another thing that attracted me at the time was a particular drawer. It was the main drawer of an antique desk placed by the window of a small Western-style room upstairs, and the contents were hardly ever taken out or tidied up, for the occupant of that room tended to be away most of the time. When opened it was full of conjuring devices, superficially elegant or ponderously impressive, the sort of things I thought belonged only either in museums or a wizard's secret cell: a twisted tube of colored glass, a rod of checkered red and green, some gaudy beads, embroidered silk handkerchiefs, a knobbly pipe, a blackish box with snakes carved on it, and so on. As I had been warned on no account to touch any of these objects while the owner was away, all I could do was cautiously run my fingers over them, swallowing nervously at the thought that I must simply put up with just looking at these things until that glorious day came when their mysterious powers would finally be given full play.

That day did eventually come, the occupant having come home on holiday. He was, as it turned out, a person of no particular distinction, but just a young uncle of mine attending medical school in Kyoto; indeed, just a friendly half-wit who was good for nothing else than messing about with conjuring tricks. Naturally enough, that wasn't the way he looked to me then, for I was quite convinced he really was a magician who could do almost anything, possessing as he did a dark skin rather like an Indian's, sharp features, and a preposterous voice which suggested some serious mental derangement. Here is a man, I thought, who has an aura of mystery about him. The voluntary muscles in his ears were also very well developed, and he could waggle them about whenever he felt like it. "Look at this, then," he'd croak, wiggling those abnormally projecting ears. There were also occasions when his ears twitched of their own accord, when he lost his temper or was feeling particularly pleased about something.

"Watch this," he told us, and with imposing gestures and a swift jerk of the waist he produced a bunch of multicolored handkerchiefs from his hand, waving them about triumphantly. He then put the knobbly pipe in his mouth, took one leisurely puff, and—lo and behold!—from the smoke he exhaled a golden chain appeared. Not only that, but the chain actually drifted in the air, with the smoke! Unfortunately, however, that bumptious cousin of mine who had often come to our house in the past happened to be among the audience at this display, and his beady eyes had soon worked out how such tricks were done.

"Huh, that's nothing," he said, with obvious contempt. "It's just tied on with a bit of string."

This aroused a childish rage in the magician, who stamped his foot in a manner quite unsuited to his years, and croaked hysterically:

"String? What string? Show it to me, you little beast! You go on telling lies like that and the devil will strike you blind, I'm warning you. Where is the damn string, then? Tell me, you cocky little pig, you lying pest! Just show me exactly where it is, because I can't see anything at all, not a thing."

My cousin stuck out his tongue, screwed up one side of his face in what was meant to be a wink, and ran off, while my uncle sat down wearily muttering to himself as he stroked his precious pipe that the boy would come to no good; and as he did so, as always in such times of stress, his awkwardly protruding ears began to twitch.

I, however, was completely taken in by the performance and admired him hugely for it, and as a consequence became a favorite of this uncle with the mobile ears, who realized that I would never make a fool of him as other children did. No doubt determined on total enslavement of this gullible boy, he used to invite me to his room and tell me lots of stories, stories too preposterous even to be called fairy tales, though I listened to them all enthralled. He must have been quite without any talent as a narrator, with the confusing habit of forgetting what he'd previously said, since an only child suddenly became blessed with brothers, or the hero who had been made immortal by the possession of a magic jewel was promptly gobbled up by a lion. He also had a bloodthirsty tendency to kill people off when the story line had become too involved or he had just run out of invention.

QUALITY
LITERATURE
from
KODANSHA INTERNATIONAL

Literature

ALMOST TRANSPARENT BLUE

Ryu Murakami/Translated by Nancy Andrew

"A Japanese mix of *A Clockwork Orange* and *L'Etranger.*"—*Newsweek*　128 pp; $5.95

THE AUTUMN WIND:
A Selection from the Poems of Issa

Translated and introduced by Lewis Mackenzie

A representative collection of classics from a haiku master.　146 pp; $5.95

THE BARREN ZONE

Toyoko Yamasaki/Translated by James T. Araki

After surviving several years in Siberian prisoner of war camps, a Japanese army officer returns to an unfamiliar Japan.　392 pp; available only in Japan

BETTY-SAN

Michiko Yamamoto
Translated by Geraldine Harcourt

"Impressive. The stories' rich sense of place weaves an unsentimental poetry from their loneliness."
—*Publishers Weekly*　152 pp; $4.95

BLACK RAIN

Masuji Ibuse/Translated by John Bester

A novel about Hiroshima.
"A painful and very beautiful book."—John Hersey
　300 pp; $6.95

BOTCHAN

Soseki Natsume/Translated by Alan Turney

The hilarious classic tale about a young man's rebellion.
"Soseki's lightest and funniest work."—Donald Keene　174 pp; $5.95

CHILDHC

Jun'ichiro Tan

"Invaluable as derful portrait *Review of Boo*

CHRONIC

Yasushi Inoue

One of Japa mother's last y "A gentle mer

A DARK N

Naoya Shiga/

A story of a family.
"One of the g ture."—*Choice*

THE DAR

Junnosuke Yos

Despite carryi ship at a time, love.
"The translati

THE DOC

Sawako Ariyos
Translated by W

A tender tale well as a comp in Japanese so "An excellent

"What happened to the magic jewel?" I asked him at one point, tentatively, it's true, but prompted by a sense of real dismay. "I thought he couldn't die because of the magic?"

An uneasy look passed across his dark, solemn face, and that perplexity which marked the moments when his conjuring tricks were seen through also cast its shadow over him, but he tried to pass it off by croaking even more impressively:

"That's right. Pretty sharp of you to notice that. Well, the truth of the matter is, the prince had forgotten all about it. Only after he'd died did he suddenly remember about the magic jewel. So he took it straight out of his pocket, rubbed it, and said the magic words; and then, wonder of wonders ..."

"But when someone's dead they can't move their hands, can they?"

My uncle grimaced, indicating by a gloomy look that I'd best be quiet, and then, after a brief pause for reflection, continued.

"He had the power of the magic jewel to thank for that. That was the whole point of it, in fact. You see, it was a mysterious power, a very mysterious power indeed. An almost incredible power, not the kind of thing you find just lying around anywhere. Practically never find anything like that; at least not that kind of really amazing, inexplicable ..."

Unable to continue he kept repeating the same thing, but he noticed the first signs of boredom appearing on the face of his captive audience, so he went on in some haste:

"The prince's heart, which had stopped beating, started up again. Thumpety thump it went, missing a beat here and there at first, of course, because it started off in a state of great irregularity, what they call *alitomia perpetra* in Latin, but now it began beating again quite normally...."

I suppose one reason why he inserted this advanced medical

terminology into the tale was that he was revising for his exams, although an underlying motive—the urge to bluff an innocent child into an attitude of bewildered respect—cannot be discounted; and the truth is I did feel impressed by the mark of authority it seemed to give the story as a whole.

"So the prince flew off to Mars, and Mars, being the red planet, is of course covered with flames all the time, and for someone coming from the cold world of the moon ..."

"But the prince had been on Venus up to now," I corrected him.

"Well, Venus is the same sort of thing. Anyway, the place was swarming with monsters with great long necks, and the prince got hold of one of them by the throat, just here...." He pointed to the place on his own neck. "This muscle here has a really long name in Latin. Ready? It's called *musculus sternocleidomastoideus*."

When the story was finally over he lit a cigarette in obvious relief, and asked me casually what I thought of it, drawing my attention—as he often did on such occasions—to the extent of his knowledge ("Your uncle knows lots of things, doesn't he?"). I nodded meekly in agreement, for I truly did believe there was nobody in the world to compare with him, and he patted me on the head in satisfaction.

"When you grow up I bet you'll become someone important. You'll be a great painter, I'm sure."

This was a reference to the fact that I was remarkably good at drawing, having had several pictures exhibited and been given a number of certificates.

"That's it; a great painter like Cézanne or Van Gogh," he added, though I doubt if he would have been able to distinguish between the two.

Yet the awe I felt in his presence was to vanish almost entirely one Christmas Eve. It all began well enough, but two appalling blunders proved to be irretrievable. In fact even the opening wasn't all that auspicious, for he made his entrance dressed in an antique cloak and top hat handed down from my grandfather which gave him a rather bat-like appearance, and he didn't look at all like the possessor of hidden, mystic powers. Even more ominous was the fact that my smart-aleck cousin had been chosen as his assistant, since no more suitable child was available. The magician himself was slightly drunk, but he still managed a few tricks using the cards and the snake-covered box with some dexterity, and there was considerable applause. The trouble was, as even he soon realized, it was his assistant's eccentric posturings that really made the audience clap. A university student, even a very friendly one, is hardly going to enjoy being upstaged by a primary-school kid, and his obvious displeasure made him redouble his efforts, with elaborate gestures and poses of his own, to get the audience's attention back.

"Now, for my next trick," he said at last, in a wheezing voice that suggested he was suffering from throat cancer, and with an extravagant flourish he produced from somewhere a brilliant gold and green glass ball. It was about the size of an apple, and was so dazzling one was bound to think that if indeed a magic ball existed in this world then this must be it.

"Ladies and gentlemen, I have here in my hand a green ball, a treasure of peerless price. So fragile is it that, if I let it fall to the ground, it would instantly be smashed to smithereens. And yet, before your very eyes, I shall stop this ball in its descent; I shall stop it in midair and maintain it there!"

"I shouldn't do that if I were you," warned my cousin in a very cool, grown-up voice. "It could be dangerous."

"Keep out of this, junior. Right, here goes!"

He let the ball drop from his hand, but the next moment all his hopes were betrayed and the incredible happened, for the ball refused to halt in midair and plunged violently to the floor, where, as he had promised, it was smashed to smithereens. The magician's consternation was pitiful to behold, but he finally managed to recover his composure, this time producing a metal cup and calling me out from the audience to assist him. What I was instructed to do was to take up a very large kettle full of water and pour the entire contents into the cup.

Another cheeky comment from my cousin—"At least there's no danger of anything breaking"—made the magician curse him roundly under his breath, while he fiddled about with something inside his cloak. But by now the cup, which he was holding close to him, had filled up with water to the point of overflowing, and when I looked into his face I could see every sign of panic, so I stopped pouring, particularly as my cousin was shouting excitedly that it had started to slop over in a voice that would have put anybody off; but the magician only urged me to keep on pouring, keep on pouring away, since this was a magic cup that could take over half a gallon, and I shouldn't pay any attention to whatever the little pest might say; and the cup did indeed start to empty, and once more I believed in my uncle's magic powers. How this was done I didn't know, although there was some sort of device that drained the cup when it was on the verge of overflowing.

Then a dreadful thing happened. There was a dull ripping sound in the region of my uncle's chest, and immediately a large quantity of water flooded down his trousers, while the cup tilted and poured more water over his cloak. This all happened in a flash and, to a storm of laughter from the audience, the drenched magician was left standing, with his ears twitching uncontrollably, in a pool of water that had formed on the floor. Regardless of what kind of spectacle he was making, he then turned with terrible loathing on my cousin and tried to grab hold of him. But the boy was too quick for him, leaping nimbly over the chairs and making his escape, shouting out in a high-pitched, jeering voice that his uncle wasn't human but a monster with wiggly ears.

The only result of all this, as far as I was concerned, was that my young uncle treated me with even greater kindness, showing me what horsetail spores and the dust from butterflies' wings looked like under the microscope, and buying me a folding net for catching insects. But all traces of the mystic magician had faded, never to return, and though I still admired him with the persistence of a child I discovered that I could take pleasure and pride in the fact that he didn't know things that I did. Quite often, for example, I would spend almost the entire day by myself simply watching swallowtails fluttering about the hedge of trifoliate orange, or observing the activities of a beetle thrusting its head inside an empty snail shell. I ran off to tell him about this last remarkable discovery, but the only information I obtained was about the unreliable nature of adult knowledge.

"What do you mean? A dor? Never heard of it. You sure it's not just an ordinary horned beetle?"

"No. A horned beetle's only got one horn, a long one sticking right out."

"That's right. It's got one horn. So has yours, hasn't it?"

"No, it's got two."

"Two? It's got two? That's the first I've heard of an insect like that. Must be a very weird and wonderful thing; a wonder of wonders, I should think."

So I went and caught the beetle and showed it to him, but he still insisted it was an ordinary one-horned beetle.

"But it's got two horns, hasn't it?"

"You're right, it has. Funny, isn't it? They all used to have only one when I was small."

He then slapped his thigh and, only wiggling his ears very slightly, declared that this must be an example of sudden mutation.

Every summer the family used to rent a lakeside house in the mountains. To be released from school and spend a month away from the city was like being in paradise, a period of absolute sensual fulfillment.

The mountains were full of flora and fauna never seen on the plains. The woods had a rich, dank smell quite unlike that of the oak groves I knew, the bark of the trees oozing with a sticky resin. In the patches of black earth among the grass one found weird mushrooms forming a ring with drooping heads. Butterflies, enormous black ones, much larger than the same kind seen near home, floated down onto the gold-banded mountain lilies in search of nectar, their four ink-black wings sprinkled with grains of gold and green, while their legs and feelers were made more bewitching by the crimson pollen with which they were covered. When I woke up during the night I could hear the deathwatch beetle behind the paper screen of the window making its small, ever vanishing sound. I never managed to discover what this beetle looked like, and it was just as if the paper itself were singing, or the cloth edges of the worn-out tatami matting. Also, in the light of the moon flowing in from the window, I would watch a daddy longlegs groping its way slowly across the wall on its threadlike legs. At times like these I would sense the cold mountain air stealing inside me through my eyes, wide open now as, half in joy and half in fear, I steeped my body in this fairy-tale world. In a mood created by the ticking of the deathwatch beetle, fading and then returning again, the spider moved the thin tips of its legs, keeping time to that evanescent music, as if a perfect rapport had been established between the two and they were now one linked existence. The slow legs crept onward, swaying to the music, until the two faded together, neither being heard nor seen, for by then I would have gone to sleep, until the time when the rim of the mountain whitened, and the sounds of the clear-toned cicadas and the turtledoves cooing told me the long night was over and the day had begun.

One day I walked along a mountain path with a butterfly net in my hand. The high summer sun deepened the shadows of the trees, and the smell of the grass dissolved into the sweat on my body. A sudden bright object flickered before me. It was a butterfly, a rare kind I didn't know; or so my experience told me, although it couldn't tell me why my knees should have trembled at the sight, and why the hand that gripped the handle of the net shook so violently.

The swirl of silver wings spun before me again, and I waved crazily at it with my net. Got it! I gazed at the four small wings beating tragically in the net's fine mesh. I knelt down and stretched my hand inside, holding it captive. Now the angel with scaled wings was lying, dead, in the palm of my hand. The silver-white dust sparkled on the outside of its wings, and a soft, dark, lustrous brown colored their inner surface.

For a moment a shock of half-recognition passed through me, something that became an actual prickling of pain. I looked closely at my prey again, but I certainly didn't recognize it, never having seen a specimen like it before, although in every way it matched my mental image of the perfect butterfly. I was sorry I had killed it so soon. I could have kept it in a glass case and enjoyed watching the sensitive, fluttering brightness of it. With a pang of regret I emptied a half-dead dragonfly out of the bamboo cage I had with me, and placed inside it the still object with closed wings, the corpse of my butterfly.

It was not unusual for a thick mist to rise in these mountains, and late that afternoon on my way home I noticed a cloud of it coming up from a valley nearby. The mist flowed swiftly, filtering through the trees and over the fences of the summer houses like a living thing. Visibly the dusk was falling, coming well before its time. From the woods the chorus of cicadas slackened in response, finally smothered into silence behind the now complete white veil. Probably because I set off running in such haste, by the time I got home I saw that there was no trace left in the box of my precious butterfly.

After dinner it began to drizzle, as if the mist that covered the mountainside had fused into little drops, falling in fine lines of rain.

"You'd better hurry up and have your bath," my aunt said.

"Already had it," said my cousin, not giving me a chance to say I hadn't.

While I had been indulging in my passion for insects, he had made a catapult out of a thick piece of forked wood. He claimed he'd be able to get crows with it. If he didn't have any luck with birds, he said, he would still slaughter every cicada in sight—it would stop all that awful racket; although he generously admitted that I might be somewhat inconvenienced if there were none at all left for me to catch. The upshot of the discussion was that we set up a target in our room so as get in some practice for the cicada slaughter, shooting away with the catapult for a couple of hours until our exasperated aunt shouted at us to stop.

The small children had already gone to bed. Some of the grown-ups had gone to a neighbor's house to talk. My aunt insisted that I have my bath and go to bed, and although the prospect made me slightly nervous I went by myself across the connecting passageway and into the annex where the bath was. The water came from the local hot spring, a constant supply of yellowish liquid pouring out with a melancholy sound beneath the dim glow of one naked light bulb. Once I was completely immersed in the water I was aware for a while of some presence, a living silence other than my own. The bathhouse was full of dull clouds of steam, drifting down ominously onto the surface of the water whenever any ripple disturbed it, and producing a faint rustling as they did so. But I perceived something beyond that, something softly, somberly falling. It was the rain.

I wondered what had happened to my butterfly, and knew I must have dropped it at a certain point where the road sloped. The thought of it lying soaked in the rain, gradually being stained with mud, made me bitterly regret its loss, the loss of something irreplaceable. I had been wandering about for days and finally found a butterfly I'd never seen before, and the chances of my catching the same thing again seemed nonexistent. Grieving over it, I lay for a long time in the bath with glazed eyes, so long in fact that when I got out I had a mild fainting fit (which had happened to me occasionally before and was probably caused by anemia) and almost collapsed. I managed to get my underwear on, and with my towel over my shoulder made my way back across the decaying planks of the passageway to the house. The planks were damp and felt cold on the soles of my feet. I sat down in a wicker chair on the veranda under the bright light of a lamp, and rubbed my feet dry very carefully. It seemed that my aunt had already gone to bed.

The veranda was closed off from the outside by long windows, and these were covered by some slightly soiled white curtains. The curtains had been drawn, but through a chink in them I caught a glimpse of something green and shining. The color was exactly the same shade as the glass ball my magician uncle had managed to smash to pieces. It started to preoccupy me, so I stood up and opened the curtain to have a look. It was nothing in particular, just an ordinary species of maybug of which there were so many in this area, attracted by the light and clinging to the frame of the window. There was nothing odd in this and it happened every night. But then I noticed next to the maybug a longhorn beetle, a speckled black cerambycid, waving its long feelers about in a very ostentatious way. Not only that, but there were a number of other maybugs clustered together, one of which tumbled with a small thud to the ground, its shards outspread. At the top of the window a moth with a repulsively fat abdomen revealed the brown undersides of its wings speckled with light blue, rubbing the glass with the fine hairs of its belly. I opened the next curtain, and here was a riot of color and movement, countless tiny moths fluttering their wings of yellow, red, and bluish black in a desperate effort to get inside. A large pale blue moth, looking like the queen of this assembly, was crawling along the frame. Then a maybug buzzed heavily against the glass, falling on its back onto the ground. Obviously a light at night attracts insects, but I had never seen anything like as many as this before. I opened all the curtains, and each window, as if by previous arrangement, revealed the same swarms of brilliantly colored creatures, not just a feast but an orgy for the eyes, too rich and varied to be taken in at once.

For a while I stood there stupefied, like a drunk incapable of focusing on one thing, following the movements of first one insect, then another. Yet I never thought of opening a window and trying to catch any of them that I particularly fancied, so dazzled was I by this carnival, in all its convolutions. More, then even more arrived through the thick bank of fog to join the throng.

After some time, I realized that I was searching among these scores of insects for some shape I recognized: the silver-white butterfly I had caught that day. I knew perfectly well that no butterfly would be drawn to that light, and wondered at the strangeness of my hoping to find it there. This thought seemed to ease my trance a little, which made me aware that my body had grown cold; I then looked again at the visitors gathered there outside the window. Most of the maybugs huddled together without moving, their rain-soaked shards folded, only their eyes weirdly shining and alive. Once I'd noticed that, I saw the moths all staring in my direction, wings trembling lightly, with their ominously burning compound eyes of emerald and ruby. I was scared enough to decide to take a pace backward, but my legs refused to move. Then something seemed to burst inside my head, like delicate fireworks, myriads of glittering eyes. My field of vision turned dark with lights and colors flickering and falling apart. I had a sense of growing remote from myself, and was aware of the enormous length of time it was taking me to bend my knees.

I could hear voices a long way off whispering something, but what they were saying I didn't know. A corner of my reawakening mind registered the fact. The whispering drew closer. I realized then that it was my name that was being called, and I opened my eyes and looked about me. In a vague light like that underwater a number of obscure shapes seemed superimposed upon each other. These shapes gradually came together, became clear; became one face and then two, those of my aunt and uncle.

The grown-ups had come back, and were picking me up.

"It's all right, it's nothing to worry about," somebody said. While my nightclothes were being put on me my young uncle, the magician, was holding my wrist, frowning and shaking his head, but when he began to make some comment on my pulse rate he was brusquely told he didn't know what he was talking about, so he let go of my hand.

Still with no idea what had happened to me I was placed on my bed. I noticed my cousin in the next bed, so heartily asleep that I couldn't help smiling. With his murderous catapult beside his pillow, one arm thrust rigidly out to his side and his mouth half open, he was snoring loudly.

* * *

Near the fence that surrounded the house in Tokyo, among the bushes at the back, there flowered from spring to summer a rather striking-looking wild plant, as tall as a grown man and with heart-shaped, emarginate leaves. What was peculiar about it was that if you broke off the stems, which scattered a white pollen when shaken, they were hollow inside, and from the soft pith they exuded a yellowish brown sap which looked like some kind of medicinal ointment.

My cousin told me that this was what they made iodine from, and he smeared some of the stuff on a fresh cut of mine. It didn't sting like real iodine, so I assumed it was a superior version of it. My cousin, however, once he had finished treating the wound, added in an exaggeratedly low and threatening whisper that I had better keep quiet about it, because if I was caught doing this I would probably end up in prison. According to him, all these plants in that area belonged to an iodine manufacturer.

This crude method of treatment worked perfectly well with most minor cuts and grazes, but on one occasion it had the reverse effect and the wound grew enflamed, festering deeper and deeper beneath the scab that had formed. Even so, I went on blandly breaking off the hollow stems and rubbing the brownish sap into it, convinced it would heal this way; but there was no improvement of any kind, and eventually the skin around the wound became an ugly dark red swelling, and when I pressed it whitish pus oozed out. The day came, of course, when, despite my efforts to keep it to myself, the grown-ups discovered what was wrong with me, and after a severe scolding I was taken off in disgrace to the infirmary. Here my wound was lanced with a shiny scalpel and sweet-smelling iodoform powder was sprinkled on it, the whole then wrapped in spotless gauze. But nobody blamed my cousin for this. It was all put down to my foolish ignorance, and he watched with great interest as I struggled to hold back my tears while the incision was made. The fact is he was clever, in the way he talked and behaved, and hardly anyone ever managed to catch him out in anything.

"Not likely to be any long-necked monsters on Mars, are there?" he said to me one day, snorting with derision. He was spinning a plate on top of a stick as he spoke. This was done with a skill a circus artiste might have envied, but there was no conjuring device involved, such as my magician uncle would have used: it was due merely to excellent coordination.

"Mars is full of Martians who look like octopuses. It's not on fire. It's got canals."

He neatly flipped the plate off and caught it in his hand, then whistled a few bars of some popular tune. This, too, was just another sort of showing off, and was as piercing as a traffic policeman's whistle. He was also very good at animal noises, had a gift for making grown-ups laugh by using certain rustic turns of phrase, performed well on the parallel bars, was skilled at hand-icrafts, and could walk over three yards on his hands. His great speciality, however, was as an escape artist called the Elusive Rat: he would bind his legs and arms elaborately with various bits of rope and cloth, and then, by a series of bizarre contortions, man-age to slip free of them. When he had accomplished this, he'd wrinkle up his nose and snarl:

"Aha, my fine jailer friends. Thoughtst thou thus to keep a mighty robber such as I within thy dungeon walls?"

By contrast, my arms were much too thin to perform any pull-ups on the bars, and the pallor of my skin was no healthy white but more a sickly pastiness. It was always a matter for wonder when I managed to use a knife without cutting myself, and if I tried to whistle, the only result of a tremendous straining of the lungs was the sound of escaping breath. I did, in fact, put a lot of effort into learning to whistle, leading to a state of almost constant pursing of the lips, so that my grandmother, in that fumbling way which went with her advanced years as she failed to find the right sounds with her sluggish tongue, told me there was something foxy about my face.

The clearer it became that I was a complete failure when compared to my cousin, the more I longed to be like him. For example, he was so idle at school he couldn't keep up in any sub-ject, and although he was two years older than me he had me do all his homework, yet any such superiority of mine paled to in-significance beside the ideal he represented. I tried to make my skin as dark as his by walking as much as possible in the sun, and forced myself to take part in rough games at school, dili-gently trying to acquire cuts and grazes in the process. I also managed to get the boys who played baseball on the waste ground near our house to let me join in, but only as a reserve most of the time, having usually to be content with being allowed to look for the ball whenever it got lost in the long grass.

Yet pure chance was to change all this for me, chance in the shape of a remarkable person, although when he first appeared there was little to remark in him at all beyond his shape, which was huge. Judging by this alone, he seemed to be well into his twenties. He delivered newspapers, and whenever he passed the waste ground he invariably wrinkled up his oily, fat face into a smile of the utmost affability, then wandered over to where we were playing. The ensuing conversation went generally like this.

"Come on," he'd say, "let's have a go. Just one hit. Come on."

In terms that made it quite clear we weren't prepared to put up with this nuisance, one of us would tell him he couldn't because we'd reached a vital point in the game. This only caused a further softening of his facial muscles, and in a tone of quite disgusting pathos, as though he alone bore all the pain and misery in the world, he'd say:

"Oh, go on, give us a chance. Just once. Just let me have one swing at it, that's all I'm asking. Here, I'll give you some of these."

He then produced a handful of sweets known as musket balls from his pocket, and gave out one each all round. Having bribed his way into our game, he stepped into the batter's box, with his bulky body dwarfing the small boy's bat he held, and, after some preliminary wriggling of the hips, indicated with a lusty howl that he was ready for action. But all he could ever do was clumsily ground out to the pitcher, and the awful wheedling would start again as he begged us to let him have one more go, just one, come on, just one, ducking his head repeatedly as he did so.

Yet, in a very short space of time, this same person had all the children who played on this empty lot completely under his thumb, and became manager of his own boys' baseball team. He stopped bowing and scraping or handing out musket balls, had the smaller players running around like slaves at his every beck and call, and hurled insults at anyone who made a mistake. How this state of affairs came about I have no idea, though perhaps it only goes to show that he really was remarkable after all.

One day our manager called us together and told us we were going to play a different style of game from now on, and what we most needed was someone who could really pitch. He himself would make the selection.

"Right. Now, you're all going to pitch at me. All of you. Ten throws each."

He glared at us forbiddingly, and this practice session turned out to be the most terrifying we'd had so far, each ball being greeted with a volley of abuse.

"What's this rubbish? What d'you think you're trying to do with the ball? Call yourself a pitcher? Fancy you're a pitcher, do you?"

Finally it was my turn. I'd never pitched in my life. I just aimed nervously at the mitt and threw with all my might. The ball seemed to be going dead straight at it, but at the last moment it swung to the right. The next one went in exactly the same way. The manager stood up, and I went cold all over. All he said, however, was:

"Okay, you can throw a screwball. Let's try one straight this time."

But I was mortified to find I couldn't throw straight. They all swung one way or the other, either outside or inside.

"Looks like you throw a natural screwball. Still, that means you'll be hard to hit. Got pretty good control, too. Okay, then, you'll be our ace pitcher."

When we were finally dismissed, our manager even saw fit to leave his skinny star pitcher, who was already almost swooning from all this unexpected glory, with a parting word of advice:

"Just watch that shoulder, now—the shoulder. Take care of it."

I can't claim that I didn't take a certain pride, at times, in my achievements at school, but it was still essentially a gloomy feeling, and I would gladly have sacrificed the whole lot in exchange for just one of my cousin's accomplishments. Only with regard to my skill at drawing did I experience something like a full, joyful recognition of my own talent. This wasn't because I'd won a lot of prizes for it, but more a delight in the subject itself, the attraction of various shapes, of the delicate variations in tone in what at first seemed to be merely one color or a simple combination of two or three, and the pleasure I felt in being able to grasp such distinctions.

One day, round about the time when I'd been chosen as pitcher for the baseball team, it was my turn on cleaning duty and I had to remain behind at school with a few others. The teacher finished his inspection and the others all went home, and I was alone in that peculiarly empty quietness a schoolroom has when the desks and chairs have been neatly lined up, sitting on a desk tying my shoelaces and gazing around me. Pinned on the wall at the back were the best drawings and specimens of calligraphy, all with the four circles indicating top marks inscribed on them. Since there wasn't room for the entire class's work, they were taken down in rotation, leaving only those judged to be the very best. That process must have just taken place, for of all the various drawings only ten remained, and among them there were six of mine, as the drawings were in six categories and mine had remained in each of them. This inspired a certainly childish but still genuine sense of satisfaction, which was bolstered by the fact that there were sixty pupils in our class.

I stretched up and looked hard at the pictures. I was aware of some other self concealed inside me; I could feel his presence had risen to the surface, making my skin tingle, and I knew that this was someone who allowed no prevarication, and he was now urging me persistently to draw something, to show what I was really capable of doing.

That day there had been a drawing class. We had been made to draw a vase in pastel, and when the lesson was over the teacher had put one lily in each of the four vases, probably for one of the senior classes to sketch during the next period. Carrying my satchel in one hand I went down the deserted corridor as if something were leading me along, then looked inside the art room on the second floor. It was empty, as I thought it would be, and there, on four different stands, were the vases quietly waiting. I crept inside, hurriedly got my drawing materials out of my satchel, and sat in front of one of the vases with its single flower. To risk doing this, I must have felt fairly sure that the teacher wouldn't scold me if he caught me there. I drew the outline of the vase very carefully, but was dissatisfied with it, and started immediately with the flower on a new sheet of paper. I made one of the petals more twisted than it was in reality, but that somehow seemed right to me.

I kept on working busily with the soft pastels, freely, almost crudely at times, rubbing the white petals of the drawing in places with my fingernail to produce a dull luster, a method I'd picked up from an art teacher at an exhibition who had done the same thing to a sketch of mine of a loquat which had been on display there. While I was doing this, the occasional footsteps passing in the corridor or the distant voices of children in the playground scarcely bothered me at all, and I began to lose all sense of my surroundings when I started working on the anthers, overripe with pollen. The vase, stem, and leaves I had only sketched in very roughly, but that seemed to set off the flower itself, which was somewhat out of alignment and overlarge as well. All my concentration went on the flower, as I was trying to achieve a delicate shade of color, consisting not only of the white of the petals with the light of dusk on them, but also the shadows cast by the stamens and pistils and even the dark green cloth which served as a background. The combination of tones was hard to get hold of, but it was this that I wanted to set down on paper. The light from the windows was gradually fading, making the various colors change each instant with it, and also, it seemed, my attitude toward the picture, for I began to feel that this impassioned labor would never reach completion. At times when I was momentarily freed from the spell under which I worked, I knew that what I was drawing and the actual lily on the stand were quite different, and that my version was becoming progressively more deformed and weird. The petals were no longer any shade of white, and it was even doubtful if the picture looked like a lily at all. But my obsession with the bizarre image I was creating remained the same, while the lily itself became increasingly commonplace and dull. If I had been a butterfly, it was on my picture that I would have settled, choking in the scent of this mysteriously colored flower, tumbling round and round amid the crimson pollen until I was steeped in it....

I had no idea how much time had passed, but I awoke from my trance to find the classroom had grown quite dark. I shook my heavy head, yawned a little, and looked at my drawing almost with indifference. It was just a rather grubby mess of colors, and my excitement of only a little while ago had completely disappeared. Yet this hopeless piece of work still had something in it that gave me satisfaction, and I folded it in two and put it away inside my satchel along with my pastels.

But I was tired, both physically and mentally; so much so that when I went out into the corridor I just felt like sitting down on the floor there and then. The experience had left an intensely empty aftertaste, and I stood at the window and looked outside. There was still light enough in the sky, but the playground was in shadow. There were no children anywhere to be seen. The very clarity of the twilight sky only made the scene more dismal. While I had been absorbed in my drawing, other children must have been having a wonderful time, playing to their heart's content. So I slung my satchel over my shoulders and went down the creaking stairs, full of a strange regret for what I'd done, and finally telling myself that I'd been wasting my time, and that I loathed pictures anyway.

Feeling chastened, I thought that one could always whistle if nothing else seemed to work, and pursed my lips to do so; but an empty rush of breath was all I could produce.

All the rich potential of childhood only resulted in my gradually turning into a perfectly ordinary boy. This had entailed an enormous effort on my part, and if I was still different in any way from the normal, healthy boy it was certainly not something that appeared on the surface. I had already learned to mimic all my cousin's skills, and pitched for the baseball team reasonably well. Occasionally, however, but only very occasionally, I did have moments which were like a form of awakening....

Yet that time when I fell over and hurt myself, I was merely enacting one more aspect of the stereotype: the plucky and enterprising sort of boy. The others were trying to capture a stronghold on a local hill, and I was determined to steal a march on them all by myself, making a wide detour though pathless thickets of tall bamboo grass to attack the enemy in the rear. Unfortunately, with my attention focused on this trivial ambition, I managed to catch my foot in a coil of grass when leaping across a small depression in the ground, and went flat on my face. I must have cracked my kneecap on a sharp stone as I fell, for it went completely numb and I found I couldn't move. When I finally managed to sit up and look at the part of myself I still couldn't feel, fresh blood was welling from a muddy wound, the blood mingling with the dirt and describing leisurely patterns down my shin. I took out my handkerchief and pressed it on the wound, but that didn't stop the flow of blood. I stared at it, distracted by the color, remembering how I often used to go to the dispensary in the hospital and be given a sweet mixture of red wine and a colorless syrup, which always seemed to me to look like blood. But what I now saw welling out of my knee was different, a substance which seemed unlike anything found elsewhere in nature, a color which even the most varied palette could never imitate.

The idea of having something quite unique in me then became focused on my other limbs, as I sensed that this body of mine was altogether a thing apart, not only from the grass and stones about me but from the other boys as well, whose voices I could plainly hear. I was overcome by the feeling that I was myself, alone, by a confused notion of independent identity; and that when eventually I stood up and went to join them, there would still be something of me that would never be absorbed into the group. The numbness in my knee had subsided, so I sat there for a long time with my handkerchief pressed to it, trying to endure the pain as it became more and more intense. Evening had spread out over the hill, and when I looked up I noticed how different was the color of that twilight sky, the color of those clouds.

Yet this moment itself faded even more quickly than the passing of the sunset hour, and when the bleeding had stopped and I went back to join in the game with my friends, I soon forgot the mysterious feelings of not long before. After a glorious hand-to-hand struggle, we ate the sweets we'd hidden in our pockets, and the caked blood on my knee became an honorable scar of which I could feel proud, like a medal won in battle. So whenever I now think seriously about the past it seems to me that, if the days and months had gone on passing in that way, I might have become perhaps, if not a professional baseball player, at least the star performer in some circus troupe; for I no longer spent hours listening to the sound of the wind in the leaves, and I had long given up gazing at insects in an attempt to work out the meanings hidden in the traceries on their wings or plated backs.

But an illness was waiting for me which was to prove to be decisive. It took me quietly by the hand and, as I grew more acquainted with it, led me back again to the world from which I'd run away. I now see this as fate, but our various fates are no doubt already there within our bodies, circulating with our blood, right from the very start.

* * *

It may seem farfetched to link the behavior of human beings to the way a silkworm, eating holes in a leaf without understanding why, pauses sometimes to raise its head uneasily; but each of us surely, at some point in our lives, has moments of that kind. Like that season on the high plains when the air is particularly clear and one can see for miles, there are times when our responses are extraordinarily alert, when our senses achieve a power which impels them to seek out the meaning of our lives in that shadowy region between the present and the distant past. What until then has seemed of little account, those things we have blithely overlooked, take on a new and lasting significance, become precious things which should be carefully guarded. Not that we have any deliberate consciousness of this, for it is something that arises in the form of intimations, of suggestions and doubts.

Often it comes as pain, bringing the smell of death with it, an illness stimulated by obsessive thoughts perhaps, but in turn stimulating other workings of the mind. The fear comes, the temperature rises, and we are given sudden glimpses of the future, so that when the pain has passed the sick man's eyes acquire a deeper clarity. Again, the body sweats and weakens, and death ceases to be something far off at the limits of life, but something always present, always underlying it. These physical and mental changes, these aspects of human life which only indicate the frail impermanence on which all of it is based, are not so much an aberration as an expression of what life in its essence really is.

Yet the illness I suffered from that winter certainly didn't come in any dramatic or alarming form; it came quite casually, bringing no fever, no loss of consciousness with it, biding its time, doing its work slowly and methodically. The kidney infection known as chronic glomerulonephritis can take weeks or months to cure; it is not all that uncommon for it to take years.

Even so, from the very outset, I felt that this wasn't my usual cold. The sheets seemed to take ages to warm up, and I lay in their unaccustomed coldness listening to the silence and trying to grasp what was happening to me. My body felt so dull and heavy it was an effort just to move, which seemed vaguely ominous, suggesting that whatever this illness might be it couldn't be something ordinary. I swallowed hard, and wondered if I was going to die, perhaps seeing a connection with my sister's death. Still, my body merely ached; I was in no pain and had no temperature to speak of, so I told myself it was nonsense to think of dying.

One morning not long before the winter holidays, however, when the heaviness of the past few days had become particularly oppressive and I was wondering whether to go to school or not, my magician uncle—of all people—became the first person to discover just how ill I was. He was due to take his final exams and had come home for a few days' rest, but was still carrying his revision notes around with him wherever he went, even in the lavatory, and this habit of his came to play a vital, if accidental part in the discovery. As soon as he noticed his nephew's puffy eyelids, an expression of intense seriousness came over his face, one that I'd never seen before. Even the most complicated conjuring trick, it seemed, had never aroused the same degree of anxious expectation in him. He immediately took a sample of my urine and, once he'd got me back into bed again, rushed off to the hospital to call in a more experienced doctor.

My older uncle soon arrived in his white coat and gave me a thorough checkup, pressing my shins and the backs of my hands a number of times, and solemnly winding the blood pressure cuff around my arm. Meanwhile, the magician was hopping about holding a test tube with some white sediment in it. "Hopping" is a little unfair, perhaps, but he was obviously in a state of high excitement, unable to hide his pleasure in the fact that, though hardly a qualified doctor as yet, he had diagnosed a sick patient with one incisive glance. So disturbed was he by it all that his ears kept up a constant wiggling, while he muttered various foreign words to himself and told the assembled children to keep quiet, although he was the only one making any noise.

Nanny, who was terribly worried about me, had been sitting at my side for some time when she asked me if I'd like some gruel, but my older uncle, handing his stethoscope to the nurse, told her I would be better off without any food, the important thing being "absolute repose." To this, the magician quickly added:

"Even when he does get some gruel, there must be no pickled plums or dried bonito in it. Anything salty, any meat or fish are quite out of the question. Or, to put it more technically, all protein and saline substances are strictly forbidden."

Big Ears was clearly reveling in his role; but it was my cousin, watching inquisitively from the rear, who as usual had the last word and caused a burst of laughter from everybody present by asking (he was already going to middle school) what "absolute repose" was.

I seem to have dozed off after that; not into the kind of sleep that comes from sheer exhaustion, nor even an uneasy slumber where one drifts between the worlds of dream and reality, but that rare condition which wraps one in a heavy stillness. Submerged like this, it seems the deeper strata of our personalities are slowly altered as some silent interchange occurs between our conscious and unconscious minds, between all we have acquired so far and what the future seems to hold, and only then do our true instincts finally emerge. At times, I seemed to be half aware of noises in the outside world, though never discovering if that was what they really were, for the soft drowsiness soon flowed back and sleep possessed my body once again. Normally I could never sleep properly even at night, but that day I drowsed right through till evening, a drowsiness which quietly washed away the irrelevant accumulations of the years, all those things I had thought I wanted and tried so hard to make my own. It was as if my soul had sent the body off to sleep in order to gain time for itself in which to learn to breathe again.

When I awoke, my surroundings were dark, with just a dull, fading light to be seen through the window. How silent the world had become, stagnant, as if time hardly flowed at all, a world in which there only drifted new premonitions of things as yet unknown. I shifted my head slightly on my pillow, feeling absurdly small, as though I'd been reborn as a baby once again; and if, for a while, I had been left quite alone I am convinced I would have remembered those aspects of my past which had vanished long ago.

But the light soon came on. Nanny was looking into my face, asking me if I wanted something to eat. I nodded, and she fed me one spoonful, then another, of some thin rice gruel. It was lukewarm and tasted of nothing. I wasn't feeling very hungry so I refused the third spoonful. I drank some coarse green tea from a feeding cup, and that tasted quite nice, though I couldn't help thinking how much better it would have been with some salt added, particularly as it was forbidden to me now. I then realized I hadn't caught a cold for two years. I recalled, with longing, the sight of a pickled plum staining the white rice a bright, fresh crimson. I indicated to Nanny that I'd had enough, and closed my eyes.

Someone else had arrived. I opened my eyes and saw my young uncle sitting by my pillow. In the kindest possible voice, he asked me how I was. It was clear from the way he looked and talked that he felt guilty about getting so carried away that morning and not being more concerned about his sick nephew. There was also the fact that he was too busy revising for his finals to have time to look after me. I tried hard to smile, then asked him in a small voice how long it would be before I could have a pickled plum. He put his hand lightly on my head.

"Well, you are seriously ill, you know. It may take a bit of time."

"How much? A fortnight?"

"Oh, I don't know. Probably only about ten days or so."

I could tell that he was lying, and that it would take at least a fortnight, probably more. I gave a nod, then gazed up at the wavy patterns in the grain of the smoke-stained, paneled ceiling.

On a number of days, snow fell outside my window. I lay and watched its infinitely slow descent, the flakes sometimes drifting up again as if time were flowing backward and controlled the way they fell. The limited view I had of the world outside consisted of the fixed line of the top of a fence, a part of the roof of the house next door, and the bare branches at the top of a ginkgo tree; and on all of them the snow fell, swirling and spinning or falling quite vertically, before it finally settled. At first it was thin and powdery, then falling in great flakes, then mingled once with hail; I had never known a year in which there had been so much snow. I remember in particular how it gathered on the branches of the tree, fairy-tale crystallizations or fantastic swellings shining in the occasional light of the sun, or freezing eerily under the ink-black sky at night. If there were to be an even heavier fall of snow, I thought, then for a while everything would come to a halt, a deep and soundless sleep would cover all the objects in the world, and even time would stop.

Yet in reality time was a very simple, constant process, which apparently maintained its even pace though nothing changed within my room, and still I felt no pain and had no temperature. The iron kettle on the charcoal brazier sang monotonously as it boiled away, and the grain in the wooden ceiling, which I gazed at constantly, remained the same. I used to count the rings in that wood a number of times each day, and idly amuse myself by tracing the shapes of animals and people among them. For as long as they lasted, I watched the patterns of brief, pale sunlight as they slowly moved across the paper screen. I just lay on my back and looked, at the transient shapes of the steam from the iron kettle, at the shadows on the branches of the tree as they altered with the changing weather. So one hour passed into another, one day was added to another day, and entire weeks went by.

The heavy, weak feeling in my body began to go, and now the one thing I looked forward to each day was my three meals. But I was still allowed no salt. There was a kind of soy sauce made without salt specially for kidney patients, but all it had was a rather weird, medicinal taste. There was something even odder called non-saline salt on sale, but the stimulus this white powder gave the palate was only very distantly related to real salt.

Nanny wrapped thick lumps of soggy rice for me in pickled cabbage leaves as she had done in the past, but boiled them in such a way that they were quite tasteless too. She would sprinkle a little artificial salt on them and pop them into my open, bird-like mouth, saying the fat one was like my great uncle and the thin one like... I didn't want to upset her so I never mentioned pickled plums, but the memory of that bitter, pungent taste tormented me even when I slept.

My cousin had restrained himself during the early stages of my illness, but after a while he began to bait me, saying, for example, on one occasion: "We're having rice curry tonight. Or is it curried rice?" He rolled his eyes about as though baffled by the question, then asked my grandmother in a perfectly serious voice if it was called rice curry or curried rice. This annoyed her so much she drove him out of the room.

Apparently, I was still quite seriously ill. My urine samples continued to reveal a large number of red corpuscles under the microscope, and they instantly transformed the milk-white reagent into muddy clouds. So I gave up my craving for sharp tastes and found a substitute in colors, the bright colors I treasured in my head: the flowers of the garden zinnia in high summer; the transparent wings of *Hexacentrus unicolor*, a grasshopper which stridulates all night long; or the stag beetle playing on the lawn.

I remembered previous summers when I had collected insects as part of my homework. Compared with the passionate energy I'd devoted to baseball at the time, I suppose I had been fairly lukewarm about it, but it was reassuring to know that my two specimen boxes still contained that rare dor with the two horns and wide, gaping jaw which had so perplexed my uncle; an ultramarine hairstreak butterfly; and an emperor moth whose wings had crimson undersides. I immediately asked Granny to get the boxes out of the cupboard. My heart beating excitedly, though still lying on my back in bed, I peered through the cold glass lids, only to find that my moth, my butterfly, and my beetle were all horribly mildewed and worm-eaten—a broken feeler here, a torn wing there.

I frowned with disappointment, deciding I must do something about it—collect new specimens and put them in a much cleaner box—but it was winter, and I couldn't get up anyway. So I turned my head toward the window and the gray sky beyond, which was threatening snow again; then sank back slowly on my pillow and stared up at the ceiling, at the dreary patterns in the wood, all of which I'd long since learned by heart.

Then one day, a day when the sun shone through my window out of a piercingly clear blue sky, a number of good things happened to me. Because the amount of albumin in my urine had gone down I was allowed to eat some fish, or at least certain parts of it, and to sit up in bed occasionally. A parcel also arrived from my young uncle, who was apparently now busy doing his exams. I opened it, and what at first sight seemed to be an incredibly dull sort of book turned out to be a children's encyclopedia of insects, full of wonderfully colored illustrations of all kinds of things. I turned the pages with trembling hands, sniffing the odor of fresh ink and gazing intently at the rarer ones, although what pleased me most was that I already knew quite a lot of the species that appeared in the book. There was a big yellow emperor moth, and a wasp with rusty wings dragging along a spider, and all three had been given their common names, as well as the scholarly ones in Latin which I couldn't read. Feeling almost dizzy with excitement, I pounced on the names of insects I was well acquainted with but had never known what to call. That gorgeous butterfly which I had often seen near alpine lilies was, according to its name, considered to be like a mountain crow, and the beetle that my uncle had called a sudden mutation was described as being of the hoe-shaped helmet crest variety. The hunting wasp that flew back and forth with burning, flickering wings across those patches of red earth was a yellow-striped tortoiseshell, and the daylight moths that bred in swarms at the back of our house in early summer were yellow-legged tussocks. It was like finally hearing, from her own chaste lips, the name of a girl whose image had been fixed in one's mind for years; and all the longing I had felt for the outside world was fully satisfied in this one book.

I turned more pages and came to an illustration which induced that same mysterious tingling in my spine experienced several times before. It was of the small butterfly I'd never been able to forget, and showed not only a view of its brilliant silver-white undersides, but one of it with pointed wings outspread, wings of a beautiful deep orange. It was called a silver-underside lycaenid, apparently not a particularly rare species. My original feelings of surprise and joy at this find were colored by a slight tinge of disappointment, partly because something I had thought uniquely precious had turned out to be comparatively ordinary, and also because, even in an illustration as detailed as this one, there was no real indication of the amazing silver glitter of the dust on its wings. I felt I had learned something I might have been better off not knowing, for knowledge can sometimes be cruel, blotting out half the radiance that surrounds the secret and unknown.

Nevertheless, I looked at the book again and again, living with it, so that almost every page was learned by heart. Certain forms, certain colors never lost their hold on me however often I saw them, and gradually, half-consciously, I realized that, all the while, there was something behind them I responded to. Without ever really knowing why, I feel I must have been trying to discern in them the outline of another shape: that shadowy place which had formed me and from which I'd come, the mother of my being.

Time flowed slowly by (though who knows how or where it went), and little by little it washed away the impurities in my body, brought color back into my cheeks; and after three months in bed I was finally able to get up. I started wandering about the house looking for things to do. There was one room in particular I often visited; it belonged to an older cousin of mine who was going to a girls' high school and had no time for boys like me, so I only went when she was out. She was an avid reader—the shelves and cupboard in her room were crammed with books—and her reading was always done to the accompaniment of tiny, apparently reluctant bites of a large bar of chocolate. Perhaps she only read as a means of coping with the act of eating chocolate.

I used to rummage through the books in her cupboard until I found something I wanted, usually a book of fairy tales with nicely colored illustrations. I had never liked reading very much, and looked for books of pictures or photographs. Sometimes I would be so struck by the picture of a knight in armor or a princess or a goblin, I would spend almost an hour looking at it. I was particularly attracted by the ruined castle in which the wizard always seemed to live, an attraction as hard to explain to myself as that of the shape of an insect. When I had finished, I would put the books back exactly as I'd found them, then make a quick retreat.

Once, I reached right to the back of the cupboard and found an untidy pile of magazines which I only managed to extract with considerable effort. They were magazines about the all-girl musical revue, something my cousin had once been very keen on. I flipped through the pages only half paying attention, although there were some quite interesting things, like the picture of lots of girls dressed up as natives in grass skirts, and even one of a prince wearing a sword on a real horse. While I was looking at these stage photos I noticed in the corner of a page a picture of a very innocent, unsophisticated-looking girl. It was a small, round portrait showing only the head and shoulders, and she was smiling in a friendly way at me with her dark eyes. At least, one side of her face was smiling happily with the tiniest of dimples, but the other side looked quite serious, and the overall impression it gave was slightly sad. I really liked that face. The longer I looked at it the more appealing it became, exerting the same obsessive hold on me that insects did when one allowed one's eyes to linger on all their delicate features. Though it was obviously the first time I had seen this face, it seemed like one I'd known for a long time, but, search as I might for some face hidden in my memory, there was nothing I could find.

Eventually I made a bold decision, though I had awful pangs of conscience about it. I cut the photo out with a pair of scissors. My cousin, in fact, had done the same thing herself on several other pages, so there was no reason to think she would notice. I held the piece of round, thin paper in my hand, trying to think of somewhere to hide it. I found an old diary in the drawer of my desk, one I'd been given two years ago as my very first diary, although I had only made entries in it for about a month, if that, and most of these were only of the very briefest kind. Above one of these entries ("Studied and played" written in fountain pen) I carefully placed the girl's photograph, then closed the dark brown covers, bending my head slightly as I did so.

After that I sometimes took the diary out and opened it at the place where the small, round picture was hidden. I had no idea why I did this; I certainly hadn't any conscious reason for it. I looked at it as once I'd gazed at insects that had caught my fancy and been put inside a glass bottle: attentively, tirelessly.

The cold night spread out around me, a living darkness swirling under the eaves of the old wooden houses of this castle town, and rising up again after my footsteps had disturbed it. It slid low over the frozen ground, collecting in patches, crowding under the feeble, naked lights of the streetlamps as if determined to put them out. All the various noises of the now sleeping town had died away, and only the suffocating air remained. I tried to walk as quietly as I could, but the sharp ears of the night never let me pass unnoticed. A grubby, off-white dog appeared out of a side alley, its tail drooping with the cold, and it followed me, snuffling at the places where my feet had trod, then raising its head and gulping at the night air several times, as if the starving beast were trying to eat my footsteps as the sounds faded upward.

I found myself walking by a ditch. The shallow water had frozen over, casting back a hollow echo of my steps, but sounding heavier and much wearier, dragging over the ground, until I realized they weren't mine but those of a deeply bent old woman I could just make out in the distance coming toward me. Every five or six paces she stopped, inclined her head a little, and readjusted her grip on her stick, as though she were listening to some faint, far-off sound; and the gesture reminded me of my grandmother, who had died some years ago.

Granny had become so very old she could hear or say practically nothing, a form of living death arousing, as if to make up for the fact that she could no longer be verbally offensive, the mild disgust that people feel when faced with anything that has gone on living far too long. Once her hair had turned completely white she had stopped dyeing it, and it looked magnificent, although it always made me think of a certain kind of very furry caterpillar. She no longer smiled, but she never got angry either, only producing a vague mumble sometimes which no one but the visiting nurse, who had been looking after her for years, could make any sense of. She used to enjoy sitting for hours in a wicker chair on the veranda, but even when she was being fed her fruit juice there she seemed to be preoccupied by something else, muttering to her trusted nurse that she had noticed a suspicious noise. I remembered the odd smell that hung about her coffin, the smell of death evading the heavy odor of the flowers and finding its way to me right at the back behind the grown-ups. I moved forward slightly, trying to make out what it was, and when one of my bones somewhere creaked a little, I can remember thinking that if Granny had still been alive and well she would have heard even that tiny sound....

The old woman came right up to me, but passed by with her

89

eyes unwaveringly fixed ahead, as though she hadn't even noticed
I was there. This worried me, since I often had the feeling at that
time that I hardly existed in the present at all. I quickly took a
deep breath of air, air so cold it tickled my throat, as if the darkness I'd breathed in with it had formed some obstruction there. I
then turned my head to watch the old lady moving away, and
her bent back, onto which the night had now eagerly climbed,
became a solid burden, with her own death secretly wrapped up
inside it.

As her final dragging footstep froze somewhere in the darkness, my surroundings seemed even colder and blacker than before. I craned my neck back to look up at the stars, but not one
was to be seen, for the night dominated those distant spaces too.
The cold stung my ears, and I noticed how my breath flowed out
white in front of me, freezing briefly into various shapes. It was
as if my own substance were escaping from my body, leaving
only the empty shell of myself for someone else perhaps to fill. I
began to think that my earlier illness might be returning, but I
was mentally too tired to deal with any problem of this sort, and
merely wandered in uncertainty.

The last dead leaves on a nearby tree began to rattle, and the
trunk of the tree next to it creaked and swayed. The wind had
risen, the winter wind that blew at frozen midnight from the
Alps across the plain of Matsumoto like a sudden apparition, rac-
ing at will about the sky to vanish when the night came to an
end. This was a particularly violent gust, so strong I thought it
wouldn't last; but it was only a taste of what was to come, for
soon the world around me was full of creakings and rustlings
and then the sound of the rushing wind. My cloak was no pro-
tection against the cold that now cut through me to the marrow
of my bones, though at least this served the purpose of reminding

me that I really was alive. I hugged my cloak about me with both arms, feeling the life come back into my legs, and stumbled with short steps down a narrow lane. If the violence of nature hadn't half revived me in this way, then I could well have spent the whole night drifting aimlessly about the town, with only my fear of the dark for company.

The wind dropped as suddenly as it had started. Now nothing moved on the face of the earth, and in this utter silence I could clearly hear the beating of my pulse. Though I knew it was absurd, I felt that countless eyes were peering at me, and I wondered when I'd learned to be afraid of the dark like this, to find it full of mystery like some Stone Age savage. Children in any age must find the dark mysterious, yet I was no longer a child but a student almost in his twenties.

I don't remember how, but I managed eventually to get back to my room, which was even darker than outside, a darkness clinging to my face, my neck and shoulders. I started groping for the cord of the desk light, conscious that my cold, thin fingers might suddenly touch something unexpected, and knowing that I'd felt exactly the same way sometime in the past. It must have been a long time ago—perhaps even something that happened before I was born.

I found the light at last and switched it on. My primitive folding bed looked particularly cold and uninviting. I could see myself lying curled up in it, trying once again to coax myself into a shallow, fitful sleep. Yet I wanted sleep; it had became a passion for me no matter how brief, how disturbed it might be by weirdly colored nightmares. I longed for it, as sleep alone provided me with dreams.

From that point in time, soon after I'd arrived in Matsumoto when the war was heading for disaster, right through the defeat and the chronic food shortages of the autumn and winter, I was ill, not with the physical illness of my childhood when for six months I suffered from a kidney disease (assuming it was only physical), but from what one can, I think, call a purely psychological affliction: the anxiety and unrest of late adolescence. It was almost as if the atmosphere of that town had infected me. The people around me were vague, unsettled beings, lacking any real life of their own. Some busily turned the corner of the street, glancing at the windows of shops where nothing was on sale, going backward and forward as if they were moving merely for the sake of pointless motion. But others were quite different, and I watched one of them, listless, sullen, hanging his head, loitering by the side of the road with hunched shoulders and biting his fingernails; and I wondered what that tasted like to him, though all I knew was that he bit his nails and stood with downcast shoulders, one hand thrust into his trouser pocket. Another moved his body wearily, then looked suddenly at his shoulder and started scratching as if he had fleas, though he seemed to have far more important things on his mind. He then bent down casually and picked up a cigarette stub which an American soldier had tossed away. An old man approached, walking uncertainly, with his head swathed in a white bandage. He was being led by a girl who held his hand but didn't look at him, merely staring straight ahead with narrowed eyes as if intent on avoiding any mishap. The old man stumbled as he was led forward, just managing to regain his balance. His legs must have been as heavy as lead, and my own felt suddenly dull and heavy at the sight.

Sometimes as I walked the streets I began to wonder if I was really living or had already died, and as night fell the fading light would press in waves upon me, the growing darkness slowly start to eat away my body. A few snowflakes spiraled down, borne there from some distant place, and abruptly my sense of who I was would dwindle and become obscure. I knew that someone corresponding to myself existed in the space I filled, but it wasn't clear if this person was really me or not. It seemed quite possible that he was just a substitute. Nervously I decided to extend some form of greeting to this stranger, and something replied in a voice that certainly came from somewhere in my body. But perhaps it was death whose voice I heard, in the lair he'd built inside me. I thought about him.

Death is undoubtedly close to us in youth, as close as it is in infancy. During the war, however, we all forgot about death as something that lies concealed within us. Death took only alien forms, came from outside us, a piece of shrapnel perhaps; we no longer understood that such things only revealed it was already there. But when the dreary peace came, it allowed us to think again about our various deaths, and in my case the musty atmosphere of an old-fashioned school was merely a suitable catalyst for the process.

One morning, a young man I knew was found lying in bed, stone cold. His friends, as if by some unspoken agreement, gathered silently around him and sat there at his bedside motionless, their faces all the same ambiguous mask as they began to talk quite casually about him, concerned not so much with the person he had been as with the death he represented; but carefully keeping off the subject, as if by doing so death itself might pass unnoticed. One of us wrinkled his nose in an intentionally humorous way, though ultimately it looked more like some primitive gesture of respect toward the mystery of it all. Another gave a tired smile and spoke about fighting the enemy in some sun-scorched part of the Pacific; for the young man now lying there, stiff and outstretched with a piece of gauze over his face, had also fought on a coral island somewhere, unconscious of this coming death and buoyant, full of life.

There was a glass vial by the pillow, apparently with some kind of medicine in it, but things like that were irrelevant now, insignificant; our lives would go on as they were, the same repetition of events until the swift years piled up and the soft skin at last hardened and proclaimed an end. I myself said nothing. Nobody else, in practice, had really said anything either, but that wasn't the point. The fact is I was afraid to open my mouth, in the purely physical sense of the phrase. I inhaled that death only through my nose, and then left. My head still felt heavy, but I raised my face to the sky, and there was a white sun floating hazily in the mist. Occasional rays broke through in places, two or three at a time; a weird, voluptuous shining.

I was aware that I was ill: not just myself, in fact, but everybody. We were all ill, and yet it was curious that people didn't seem to care, neither the woman sitting alone in the empty shop, nor the man awkwardly gripping his knees in the streetcar. Only the children seemed capable of understanding the change that had secretly taken place in them, and at times, as dusk was falling, I would hear their voices in the streets, snatches of conversation or solitary cries that were both threatening and afraid. Those voices would remind me of my own childhood fears, and far-off sensations would revive again, rise to the surface of my skin, crawl about the thin pulse in the back of my hand, clinging to my fingernails; or reawaken in the shadow of the door and lie in wait beside my pillow. Had the grown-up world forgotten all these things? If so, then was it right that I, now old enough in years, should go on thus remembering?

But I also remembered, off and on, to go to school, and sat on a hard chair in a classroom with no stove listening to the teacher, who looked as if he wasn't getting enough to eat. It appeared to be German he was teaching, and mechanically I took down in my notebook the various things apparently relevant to higher education that he wrote up on the blackboard. All my faculties seemed to be in decline. In our class, for example, there were pupils more philosophical than Kant, more poetic than Homer, more eloquent than Theophrastus, or so it seemed to me, for they all read very difficult-looking books while I pored over the adventure stories in boys' magazines. I read about Mars. I'd known for some time that there were no long-necked monsters on the planet; nor did the Martians look like octopuses. What now existed in their place was a highly advanced species of ant men, who flew to earth in spaceships and captured human beings. The earthlings, though, were no pushover, and managed to blow up one or two of their rockets. Despite their superior technology, it seemed rather incredible that the ant men had no weapon more up-to-date than the rake. They were also only the same size as earthling children, so it appeared they were doomed to defeat in any hand-to-hand struggle. But that wasn't the end of it, and soon—look out!—from behind a quietly opening metal door another group of ant men was emerging, three times the size and with rakes five times as long, the soldier ants!!!... I found all this hilarious, but though it helped to know that one could always laugh at things, it didn't do much, in fact, to raise my spirits.

I took a more active part in the work of transforming our playground into a plowed field, and when that was over each day I used to wander into town, observing people going earnestly about their business or just watching the crowds in the black market. I often thought, when I was small, how I would at last be accepted by people when *I* was grown up, too, but now I was actually approaching that age my sense of alienation from them all became, if anything, even deeper. Trying to ignore the heaviness in my head I walked faster, feeling like a puppet under somebody else's control. I remembered having this feeling once before. It was like a child flying a kite, so passionately absorbed in it that he goes on until the light begins to fade, even though he's terrified of the dark. The kite is about as big as he is, and the cold wind tugs at his collar; and then he notices the world about him and begins to drag down the kite, floating high up in the sky. With one eye on the darkness gradually closing in, he feverishly winds and winds the string. The string tangles, caught perhaps in the withered grass of the wide field, but he goes on winding and winding without end, and the string keeps appearing endlessly out of the surrounding dark. He bites his lip to hold back the tears and keeps on winding, urgently, despairingly, almost as if the string were moving him. And I felt the same thing now, when all that mattered was to keep on moving, moving one's arms and legs.

My physical condition was obviously deteriorating. A small cut began to ulcerate, and each time I changed the bandage the scab would come away with it, revealing the moist affected part which was clearly getting worse. It was impossible to get hold of any proper medicine so I smeared some brownish herbal ointment on it, which reminded me of the iodine plant my cousin had taught me about. I threw the pus-stained bandage onto the fire, and as it smoldered I smelled the vague stench it gave off, feeling a sense of utter hopelessness from which, in a warped sort of way, I even derived a certain pleasure.

Then night would finally approach, heavy, sleepless, yet still overwhelming. Often at midnight I would open the window and

96

look out at the frozen darkness. Under the faint light of the stars, objects stood trembling, waiting for nothing. They seemed exactly like myself. On nights like these the living pretended they were dead, while the dead often seemed alive.

* * *

A wide and desolate plain. A dubious light drifts in the sky, and the shore which runs on beyond the forest is obscured in the haze. The whole plain is covered with high grass, damp and fecund, all abnormally tall, and when I brush against it huge drops of dew as large as ground-cherries fall and scatter. This wet expanse of grass flows on like waves into the distance, and I part the stems with my hands or step between them, walking on and on. My hands and feet feel light and heavy at the same time, as if I were crawling along the bottom of the sea. Then I lean over and pick up a piece of stone lying at my feet. It has a whitish, attractive shape, and is relatively soft so that when I rub it a powder easily comes off. I notice there are lots of such stones around me. There are gray and red ones as well, some half buried in the earth. I pick up three or four that I like, then look up and am surprised to find that I am standing right in front of an enormous, castle-like building. It resembles an illustration of a wizard's den I once saw in a fairy story, but when I blink my eyes it seems far less impressive, merely the shell of a crumbling structure made of brick. Mist-like creatures flow in through the dark entrance, and I follow them, now feeling strangely excited as all the indefinite objects that enter my field of vision keep changing into something else. I am standing in a large hall, but it is crowded with various furnishings and ornaments, including a huge black desk, and all these seem to spin and swirl in the weak, flickering light. A large mirror leans against one wall reflecting the dull glow, and there is a thick carpet on the floor, boldly dyed in

97

certain mysterious patterns. At first sight the whole scene appears without color, although in fact it is full of the most subtle tints and shadings, much like an early lithograph by Redon. In the far corner of the room, which is raised a little higher than the rest, a blurred white shape has appeared. I feel some powerful attraction drawing me toward it, but when I try to approach my legs won't move. I peer at it, and it becomes a naked body in a silver-white cloak, and just like a young cicada emerging from its husk the body stretches up and then bends back; at which point the figure disappears and everything about me starts to ripple, waver and fade, all outward forms—the walls, the furnishings—falling apart and vanishing like mist. Only the large mirror remains, and it seems to be coldly observing me. I stare into its clear glass, but I am not reflected there; only a dim phantom swaying and trembling.

My surroundings are growing dark, filled with a hushed sense of gravity, and the restless shadows gradually grow still, just as the troubled surface of water finally becomes calm. A bleak, funereal scene now greets my eyes: towering trees, a maze of intricately winding hedgerows. When I see dozens of headstones and wooden grave tablets I realize it must be a graveyard. In the very center is a vague half-light where, behind some railings, someone is standing by a stone column. At first it looks like a statue, or, if a human being, then someone foreign, but on closer inspection this proves to be wrong. I find myself gazing at its face, unable to look away. The face is quite unknown to me, but never have I seen one so perfect, so infinitely appealing. I am moved, not so much by its beauty, but by the conviction that this neat, slender face has been created especially for me, made as it is out of these specific lines, these particular curves with their uniquely delicate light and shade. The person's age, even at first the sex, is not clear, a mixture of girlish yet sometimes boyish features, but the slim build and thick hair falling to below the shoulders show that this must be a

girl. As she moves away from the stone column she has the severe, sur-
realistic air one sees in early religious paintings, and her face has the
pallor of something born underground not long ago. But that is only
momentarily, for as I look the blood rises in her cheeks, and a deep
smile, wonderfully alive, forms on her face. I stand immediately before
her and stare at her extraordinarily black eyes, the tiny dimples, and
the half-open, softly swelling, dangerous red mouth. An almost for-
gotten shiver of delight runs through me. I want to say her name but
don't know what to call her, and for a moment a cold shaft of sadness
slides through my heart. Now the world around me and within is all
breathing, twining together and murmuring, flowing onward in wave
upon wave....

Then I notice the girl is no longer there. In her place are rays of
light breaking down the semidarkness, and gradually the whole be-
comes bright. I am in a forest with deep green shadows, and round
about me sport all kinds of elegant beasts and birds and butterflies.
The young buds have begun to open, shedding their down, and the
birdsong I can faintly hear reminds me of some music I have heard
elsewhere, a melody of diminished semitones. I feel the joy of re-
acquaintance with some distant memory, as if my heart were filling
with fresh hope. Then I approach an ancient tree and lean against its
scarred and pockmarked trunk. A maybug is clinging to the bark. It
has blue-green shards which the light makes shine like jewels. It be-
longs to a species as yet unnamed. I have seen it once before and never
forgotten it so I can't be wrong. I slowly reach out, shaking with ten-
sion, to seize the insect ... only to release myself from a dream from
which I hadn't wished to wake.

All that confronted me when I opened my eyes was the same
pitch-dark room, at several degrees below zero, and nothing of
the scenes I had just glimpsed. But the trembling in my heart
continued, and in the dark still far from dawn I found I was

talking to myself, reliving the same simple feelings of that time when I'd been obsessed with the world of tiny six-legged creatures:

"*Anomala daimiana*—that's what it was, I'm sure—not part of some other species."

I had only started collecting insects systematically when I recovered completely from my long kidney illness. The actual catching of them was thoroughly enjoyable—pursuing the hairstreak butterfly, for example, as it fluttered in the branches of the broad-leaved trees, or pouncing on the longhorn beetles that swarm among the umbels of alpine flowers. It was what came afterward that was the problem: not carefree pleasure, but hours of grueling work, for which I had only myself to blame. With my homework for the next day's lessons still not done, I used to stay up till late at night sticking the fragile coleoptera onto celluloid slides, then writing their names neatly on labels, pausing sometimes to wonder why I was putting myself to all this trouble. Yet my patient efforts did eventually result in the accumulation of a large number of specimen boxes, among which was my prize display of gold cockchafers. Classified according to their genera and subgenera, and meticulously arranged in thirty boxes made in Germany, they were much too splendid for a mere schoolboy's collection. One day I was investigating their ontogenetic mutation, looking in particular at a couple of dozen cherry chafers, or Anomala, when I noticed one whose hair color was slightly different from the others. I examined it more closely, and decided it wasn't just a variety of the same species, but unlike anything in the whole Anomala group. It was probably a new species. *A new species!* No phrase can be more dazzling for the amateur entomologist. Unfortunately it seemed to be female, or at least I could discover no distinctive male organ anywhere, and since I only had the one insect I felt nervous about sending it off to a specialist for confirmation. The label informed me that I'd found it in the Tama hills out to the west of Tokyo, and I went there a number of times to look for another, but with no success.

That was all ages ago, however, seeming infinitely more distant than it really was in actual years. As the war continued, things like insect collecting became quite impossible, and on that unforgettable night when the great duralumin birds passed overhead and my uncle's house was burned to the ground, my whole collection vanished with it. When the nightmare of endless flames finally died away and I stood in the still hot ashes and looked around at the blackened waste, I could just make out the shape of the room we had used for storing things. My father's remaining books had been there (most of them had already been donated to a library), along with about a hundred boxes of specimens, and now it was all a heap of pale gray ash which covered even the twisted iron grilles of the windows fallen down among it, and my rare maybugs had become a handful of dust. Water from the exposed pipes dripped onto the scorched earth, tracing a few irregular lines in it. The adults called out to me, and I walked away, first picking up the battered remains of a steel helmet which I found lying at my feet. What I felt at the time was not so much grief or regret but something much harder, much simpler, much closer to the skin: a sense that a decision had been made for me, that everything was over, and the conclusion to be drawn was that any obsession for things on my part, any commitment, was only a pointless assumption of burdens which could lead to nothing but failure and defeat.

Time, in subjective terms, does not advance with the regularity of a clock but can move extremely slowly or at tremendous speed; and my recollection of that insect then was of an object from a very far-off past which I was actually in the process of forgetting. So I was astonished by the waves of memory that one brief scene in a dream could arouse. Half automatically, almost unawares, I found myself trying to recreate the dream in its entirety before it slipped away, wanting to solve some riddle of the past I felt was concealed in it.

Almost immediately an image did return, of the girl's face with my forehead so close to hers they almost touched; a scene so clear I even felt a slight embarrassment at my behavior. I also began to think that the face wasn't completely unknown to me, that another I knew only too well lay hidden in it. And yet this groping about in my memory, already tentative enough, wasn't helped by the fact that the vital dream image itself had begun to fade, and the more I tried to bring it back the fainter its outlines grew, until the edges of the picture disappeared altogether. At this point, however, when all seemed lost, the misty shape of her eyes and nose remained, only just visible yet seeming to suggest the other image that I sought. But this interchange—between one image I barely retained and another I couldn't quite grasp—was too tiring to pursue, and I must have drifted off to sleep again. Then suddenly I cried out and my eyes opened, either because the first face had reappeared in sleep or because the other had revealed itself. I was sure, at least, that I'd finally seen a face which played an essential part in my life, and that it was more human and childlike than in my dream. More than that I didn't know, for it was already gone again.

Yet the sleeping layers of my memory had been stirred by this, and recollections of other more recent events which had been on the point of fading reemerged, not just one but two or three, as if a light had been switched on. They overlapped each other as they rose to the surface of my mind, despite their having occurred at distinct periods in my life and having differed in their length and importance; for they were all connected with a few specific people who shared certain traits, and these tended to merge together in hindsight to form a composite image, however varied its components. The reader should bear this in mind as I talk about this girl, this boy, this girl....

I had been assigned to a room on the upstairs floor of the finishing shop. The clatter of belts rotating, of lathes and milling tools, reached us from below as a subdued rumble, producing a peculiarly dreamlike sense of quiet, which was only broken by the sound of schoolgirls, who had also been drafted to work there, chattering to each other in voices everyone could hear when the rasping of their files was interrupted for a while. They wore overalls of drab khaki, with a cloth showing the crimson disk of the sun bound around their foreheads, and sat in long rows at their work benches. Part of our job consisted in going around each section of that room once a day with boxes full of metal plates, and yet we had surprisingly little contact with the girls. If anyone did manage to approach them, he'd be called into a dark corner of the changing room and bawled out for being "effeminate."

In spite of this my eyes were often shyly drawn to one girl sitting at the extreme left of her bench. Normally her oval-shaped face was completely expressionless, as if she had only just woken up and remained in a sort of trance, and when occasionally she glanced about her she seemed to be quite unaware of her surroundings. With slim, almost bony fingers which looked too delicate to hold a file, she worked so slowly that one could easily have thought she was in fact asleep but with her unusually dark eyes still open. Yet even this masklike face could change in various ways, depending on the time and place. Seen from one particular angle it had an expression of faintly mocking mischievousness, and when the girl sitting beside her smiled at her it suddenly came to life, with deep dimples making her almost look as though she were sucking in her cheeks. And the sound of her laughter had a slightly nasal twang to it, giving the impression she had something wrong with her tonsils or sinuses, which for me only made it more attractive. All this conspired to produce a strange bashfulness in me, as if the vague unease and embarrassment I'd felt at middle school when passing by some girl or other had at last found a clear object to focus on.

Naturally enough I came across her at other places from time to time, on a corner of the stairs, in front of the time clock before and after work, or on the streetcar going home; and while sometimes I had expected these encounters, I was often taken completely by surprise. But, though this might sound like the beginning to a true romance, nothing really happened; in fact, all it had to offer was clear evidence of the extreme cowardice of one pathetically weak-willed youth. I didn't have the feeling that I particularly wanted to get to know her, nor even the opposite idea that I should try to restrain this feeling. I hadn't a clue what I wanted. The love I seemed to feel was simply the timorous confusion of a painfully frustrated heart.

Eventually, early in winter when the B-29s had first begun to leave their vapor trails high up in the sky, this girl who had aroused in me a medley of emotions without ever knowing what grief she caused, left the factory. The girls were being sent to work in a branch factory far away. I did see her once after that, just once. It was during the lunch break one day, as a group of us were walking near the factory gates. A truck which had just finished unloading was on the point of setting off again when a few schoolgirls on the back of it began shouting excitedly at someone to hurry. Out from the factory gates burst the girl I loved, carrying a large but apparently light cardboard box in her arms. She very nearly ran straight into us, but managed to swerve at the last moment, and her elbow, sticking out on one side of the box, brushed against my arm (I happened to be at the edge of the group). I felt an awful tightening in my chest, making me quite forget the vow I'd made to keep this secret passion to myself. I turned around and watched her as she stretched out her slim, golden brown arms and passed the cardboard box to a girl on the truck. Her arms were then seized by the others and, with cries of cheerful laughter, she was pulled on board. I watched that, too, as I watched her just managing to keep her balance as the truck started off by holding on to the shoulder of a friend, and I watched her slightly flushed face swaying from side to side. Somebody whispered something in my ear but I didn't hear what he said. Right up to the point where the truck, lurching often on the bad road, had gone far into the distance, and the figure of the girl had become small and toylike, then, bending sideways, had disappeared from sight, I stood there in a daze but with my eyes still fixed in her direction, despite the danger of my precious secret being revealed, and the fact that I would rather have died than let that happen.

So the image of the girl in khaki overalls lingered in my memory, though gradually merging with another, thereby undergoing minor alterations and distortions without my noticing they were taking place, until finally it was superimposed on that of a boy who had attracted me some two years earlier.

It was a very small thing that started it all. Round about the time when the mobilization of schoolchildren for factory work was just getting underway, the boys in my year at school, together with the year below us, were sent to a car factory for a fortnight. Nobody wanted to be put on warehouse duty since it was particularly heavy work, and one morning I had managed, as head monitor of the third year, to persuade the foreman to have our second-year students assigned there, so we were all happily sitting about in twos and threes on the log piles in the main yard waiting for work to begin. I myself was actually lying on my back, when I happened to overhear a nearby conversation.

"I suppose you keep on about going to the warehouse because he'll be there. But he hasn't come today."

"He'll be here soon. He's always late."

"Don't tell me you've been checking what time he clocks in? He's not all that much to look at anyway."

"You don't know what you're talking about."

"Come off it. What's so special about him?"

Before long, "he" apparently turned up, for the two of them started giggling, with a good deal of nudging and scuffling as well. It was the first time I'd heard anyone in our class gossiping about a junior boy, and I was completely mystified by it, so I turned my head to look and saw a smallish boy I didn't know running briskly to join his friends, who were falling in a little way off. He had a pale, thin face, was breathing rather painfully as he ran past, and otherwise seemed perfectly ordinary. I let my head sink back onto a log and decided to think about insect collecting instead, which I was still passionately interested in at the time.

A few minutes passed, and I became aware of someone standing in my vicinity, so I sat up again and saw it was the same boy.

He looked quite different at close quarters: sensitive, and rather decent.

"Are the second-year students on warehouse duty today?"

He fluttered his long eyelashes as he said this, and twisted the work gloves in his hand as though the question took a special effort on his part to ask. I assumed his group had sent him over as a punishment for being late. I could sense that the two boys who had just been debating this one's merits were somewhere nearby nudging and poking each other in ill-disguised excitement, and I suddenly felt flustered, as if it was I who had a crush on him, so I just grunted a vaguely affirmative reply.

He raised his eyes and glanced at me, and for a moment I was dazzled.

"You mean it's already been decided, has it?" he half stuttered, probably because the others had insisted that he try to get the order changed.

"Yup. All decided," I answered curtly in one breath, but he went on standing there awhile, showing all the charming confusion of a small child, and apparently wondering if he shouldn't perhaps say something more. Eventually, he gave a sharp little nod to close the conversation, though he obviously realized that he hadn't done this very gracefully, for as he turned away his cheeks were dimpled with embarrassment and a blush suffused his pale skin.

A few days after our session at the car factory had come to an end I happened to meet him in the corridor at school. He was standing by a window chatting and laughing with some boys from the same class, with a notebook in his hand which he kept rolling and unrolling. At first I just noted casually that this was the boy they'd been discussing in the factory yard, but as I walked by I felt a painful fluttering in my chest, and for no reason I could understand I almost broke into a run. And from then on I found the image of one slim little boy kept preying on my mind.

This was abetted by the fact that it was arranged that my class and his should drill together, for when one saw him bundled up in cadet corps khaki and equipped with a rifle and sidearm he looked even more remarkably like a girl, the dreary outfit only serving to show off to an almost pitiful extent the gentle elegance he naturally possessed. I was obliged to perform as platoon leader in our class, something I had always found a strain, and this new situation merely made it worse. Once, for example, when he was standing stiffly to attention, I was so distracted by the pathetic expression on his face that I gave exactly the opposite order to the one I'd been instructed to give. Immediately our warrant officer, known affectionately to us all as the Mildewed Ear, howled out that I'd been awarded five black marks. The man himself was of a sloppy appearance that hardly suited his profession, but he had a passion for putting down black marks in his little black book at the slightest provocation, and this nasty habit was made nastier by his having the marks verified and read out aloud by some other pupil. His face would flush with rage on these occasions, although he was secretly enjoying himself enormously.

"I'm telling you no lie, soldier boy—five black marks it is, recorded here in my little black book," he growled in a ridiculously deep-chested rumble. "Come on, then, let's have someone out here and take a look to make sure. You—you'll do. Double out here and read it!"

As if the whole scenario had been worked out just with me in mind, the volunteer ordered out of the ranks was the boy in question. As soon as he was pointed at, he stepped forward and ran straight toward the Mildewed Ear, staggering under the weight of his very heavy-looking rifle. Then, as though daunted by the task, he peered into the book and read out "Five black marks" in a feeble voice which contained only a trace of the harsh military tone we were expected to produce.

"Read it louder, can't you? The name as well!"

I watched him, his face contorted with the effort, as he moved his tiny lips again and gave a hopeless imitation of a shout. Since it was all his fault, doubly his fault indeed, I felt justified in trying to feel a proper sense of outrage, but I knew perfectly well it was beyond my power to hold anything against him.

Yet the hold he had over me also eventually faded. As the war went on I gradually spent less and less time at school, until that time became none at all, and though, right up to the final separation, I was bound to bump into him occasionally in the school grounds, I found it scarcely bothered me at all, having almost completely forgotten the strange emotions he had once aroused in me.

It was early in the evening. I stood for a while leaning against the hedge by the gate, but finally took the gravel road that led past our door into town. I had *geta* on my feet, too large for me and with loose thongs, and I kept feeling they were about to come off, so I had to scuff them along as though my legs were stiff. The gravel rattled and rasped, and sometimes bits of it got stuck between my bare toes. The roofs of the town jutted out in places into a western sky which was a pale yolky color, while the clear blue that still hung peacefully overhead looked as if it were being swallowed into the yellow light beyond. As I watched, however, the whole sky seemed to sink back into some enormous shadow, and I felt that I too was falling into that dark void.

Up until then I had been sitting at Nanny's bedside. She'd had a stroke two days before and was still in a coma. I had sat with my knees pressed together and watched as the thin, sharp, shiny needle was jabbed into her arm, one of those flabby arms which had gently rocked me to and fro when I'd woken up in fear and trembling from the terrors of the night. I had sat listening to the low, rumbling snores that issued from her pallid, dry, thick lips, sounding as if they were her dying breaths. I had never heard anything like it before, and couldn't get used to it. A small fly kept trying to settle on the loose folds of her face, but, each time, it seemed to hesitate at the rumbling coming up from the depths of her throat, and flew away, and then returned. I tried to drive it off with my hand, but in its nervous, willful way it always managed to come back, having caught, no doubt, the smell of death that already lurked inside her.

Now, as I dragged my feet along the ground, I reflected that there was nobody left in the world who actually loved me. I didn't have to think of how she had been an indispensable refuge for me, of how she had wrapped me in a cloak of gentleness which kept me from the harshness of the world outside, for these were things I felt—not in my mind—but on my skin.

At some point I had reached the main road, and immediately in front of me was a bus stop where a number of people were waiting. I looked at nobody in particular, but I happened to notice one person standing there and, despite the fact that I was still in a kind of daze, my mind registered the sight with immediate precision and brought me to a halt.

She was a girl of fifteen or sixteen dressed demurely in school uniform. She was swinging a rather grubby canvas bag with red borders in one hand, and biting her lower lip slightly as she looked up at the bus, which was just approaching. In the last rays

110

of the sun the soft, brown-tinged waves of her hair burned a bright auburn, while the half of her face that caught the dying light had an innocent openness which was contradicted by the other, more melancholy side. As she moved forward to board the bus her face was shown in half profile; and suddenly I remembered the photograph, the one I'd cut out of the magazine in my cousin's cupboard, that round portrait which I hadn't seen for years.

The bus was crowded. She had to squeeze between the shoulders of two people to grab hold of the bar by the entrance, and when the bus lumbered heavily away she had just managed to get her feet on the step, with the upper half of her body arched backward, which revealed the delicate ripple of her spine at the nape of the neck as an undulating shadow on her skin. I felt a shiver pass along my own spine, something I'd felt at other special moments in the past.

… The darkness grew no lighter, only deeper, and the cold caught at my ears, froze my feet, and crept inside my collar. In a state between sleep and waking, only my eyes were truly alert, filled with the lost images so miraculously restored to life— particularly those of the small cut-out photo and the girl clinging to the bus.

An expert in the interpretation of dreams would have been able to go further back into the past, into the hidden recesses of the unconscious. But I was too ignorant, and too excited by what I had already found; and, for once, a heavy sleep took hold of me. Yet even in sleep my heart was restless, so that it was still pitch-dark when I woke up. It seemed like the living darkness of the womb.

Morning came with overcast skies, with the feeblest of white light, though it was just enough to dispel the night. Every joint in my body ached, and my head felt as if it were wrapped in tight, damp cloths. But that was usual with me every morning. What was different about today was a sense of pleasant renewal at the center of all this lethargy; the result, I thought, of remembering the past.

Like a lingering tremor of that night's sleep, an idea—a question, rather—occurred to me. Do memories ever really die? I had certainly forgotten about the girl's photo, completely forgotten it. Yet if that was so, why was I now remembering not just that round scrap of paper but also myself in the act of cutting it out, and even the feeling of guilt I'd had at the time? If forgetting was not loss but only burial, a mere sinking below the level of consciousness, then things forgotten could be retrieved, even perhaps everything in one's past. They were lost only because we thought they were. If what had vanished could reappear out of the distant past as it had done in my dream, then those blank spaces before I went to school, the secrets I longed to know but couldn't discover, the whole of that deep gulf which I hadn't yet been allowed one brief glimpse into, could all conceivably be restored.

I stood up, unable to sit still, and paced about the room like a bear. I even felt like banging my precious head, with all those memories crammed inside it, against a lampshade or something to get them out. Eventually, I went back to my desk, and began thinking about the structure, the gestalt, of memory. I thought of an iceberg where the part above water was one's everyday memory; but when one's eyes were closed at night and capable of deeper vision, the iceberg began to tilt and sway, and what had been submerged appeared briefly above the surface.

That image, though inadequate, seemed true enough to me. I

then noticed, in one corner of my untidy desk, a small, cheap alarm clock. The clock had always been there, but because I'd never bothered to wind it up the object had had about as much significance for me as a lump of stone. Now that it had caught my attention, though, I picked it up, still thinking about the iceberg; and I found that, absentmindedly, I must have wound the thing because it began, after who knows how long a silence, to tick: minutely, monotonously, precisely.

* * *

Quite soon afterward the icebound season began slowly to break free and change. One afternoon I noticed sparkling motes of light dancing along the borders of a ditch, and in the west, beyond the town, the shapes of the distant Alps glittered white in the haze, with one pale, thin line of cloud and then another drifting in this direction.

I stopped at a street corner and listened. The faint sound of music came from one of the houses. The melody rose again, the soft, mournful tones of a flute, and then what seemed to be a harp and oboe joining in a flowing harmony. As far as I could tell I hadn't heard the piece before, and yet somehow I felt sure I recognized it. I listened more carefully, standing by the fence. The sound of a horn now wove its way into the muted flow of the strings, scattering one note after another, until they merged together; and with a numbness welling up in me, a fainting feeling I remembered from before, the music gradually approached a passage that I definitely knew, and felt was truly mine. At the same time, I remembered with great clarity an illusion I'd often had when young, one rich in colors and smells: of a landscape, part of a dream which must have meant a good deal to me then.

The sky is brilliantly clear, so clear there is a certain darkness to it. I am lying in a field of grass surrounded by trees. Luxuriant foliage, the bright green of early summer almost oozing from it, is fringed with clustered flowers where honey-seeking bees and gadflies sway. The sun pours down upon their wings, as on the gradually deepening leaves, the rich, swollen soil, and the various mushrooms growing there which droop their heavy heads. A larch wood not far away lies swathed in the moist, bluish light, and the sweet scent of sawdust seems to reach me here. Near me are a number of silver birch trees with slender trunks, the pure white bark peeling in places to reveal the darker wood beneath in vivid contrast. A light breeze passes, making the leaves tremble, a fluttering which moves from branch to branch, then to the very tips of them. The rustle of leaves, the burr of the wings of gadflies and bees, and the singing of birds all come together in faultless unison, a melody constantly changing as the varied plain-song of the natural world reforms in different patterns to produce this astonishing sequence of harmonies. A beetle falls from a leaf, spreading its shards and spinning through the air, and that high whirr becomes the cheerful tremolo of the clarinet, the nodding bunch of tasseled flowers providing the intermittent accompaniment of the harp.... One beautiful butterfly keeps flying just above my head, until it rests at last on a mossy tree stump. It opens and closes its wings as though it were quietly breathing, and the pattern concealed in their dark blue background burns like phosphorescence. Then I remember: I remember when I was first given a butterfly net and discovered this same magic butterfly on a mountain path. A pale band showed on the surface of the wings when it flew, producing a flickering in the air whose strange beauty fascinated me. When the butterfly folded its wings, that special radiance vanished, looking to me as if some actual magic had taken place, a phenomenon so mysterious that when I succeeded in catching it with my net I felt afraid to touch those wings in case they had poison on them. But it was only an ordinary nymphalid, and when I had learned its name and had a number of them in my specimen box the fascination died away, leaving no trace behind.... Now seen again, however, opening and closing its wings in the sun, shimmering in the same way as long before, its beauty is of a different kind. And a similar change occurs also in the trees, the grass and insects around me. As one color fades it is replaced by a more brilliant shade, and as one musical phrase expires it transforms into something still more sonorous. The veils of the secret are being removed one by one, and, each time, a more striking luster spreads over the leaves, the mushrooms ripen, are overripe, and scatter their spores. The beetle whirls its shards, the blue butterfly glitters and moves its wings, as both accompany the scales being played upon that flute, a music calling from another world still hidden behind a curtain. The woodpecker knocks on a tree trunk, a sharp percussion to release the spirit of the tree, and for a moment, for one bar of music, there is a difference in the sound, the light and color, a fullness of true sensuality. Time seems to stop in that full moment, or turn upon itself, or even become entangled in the objects of the world. Thus one more veil is taken down, and all my secrets are now scattered through my dream, and the scenes so long sought after are on the verge of being revealed, though still in the wavering form of things not yet complete. And so the varicolored phantoms fade and disappear....

I was still leaning against that fence as the cello and flute were holding the melody in the half-broken phrases that brought the music to a close. I became aware of my surroundings again, a shabby huddle of houses near the middle of town, a telegraph pole with a film poster stuck on it, and a road across the way where men and women were passing to and fro. I also noticed a nymphalid flexing its wings on the bank of a ditch by the roadside, perhaps the one piece of reality in all the copious fantasy I'd

115

just experienced. It glowed like a strip of brilliant ribbon in the sunlight of an almost springlike day, but though I tried to remember what it was called, I couldn't even think of its common name.

After somehow surviving the winter, it must have just woken up. Now its wings were completely still, revealing their bark-like undersides, though they seemed no less beautiful to me. Finally it was disturbed by the rumble of a passing cart, and flickered away over the roofs like a dart of lightning.

That mysterious music had changed me, giving new life to my melancholy days, as the spring sunshine had given to the sky. Obviously the mere change of season was one reason for the cure now taking place, but something much more deeply rooted in my heart must have been the real cause. The fact, for example, that I should have bothered at last to wind that clock after my remarkable dream seemed to indicate a wish, unconscious perhaps, to participate again in the time scale that other human beings had created.

I also got to know a particular person through the medium of that piece of music. One night when spring had at last really come, I was just lolling about in my room when I caught the first bars of a tune I soon recognized. It seemed to be coming from a room just across the corridor, which belonged to a medical student. According to what I'd heard he was almost thirty, had been studying literature at university before he went into the army, and had made a belated switch to medicine when the war ended. Although we were living in the same lodging house I had never exchanged a single word with him, and it took me some time to pluck up the courage to go and visit him, but he was surprisingly pleased to see me and even invited me inside. In one corner of the hopelessly untidy room was an old portable gramophone, playing the same music I had heard and now reaching the end of the record.

"Sorry about all this mess. Anyway, sit down somewhere. Luckily I happen to have a good supply of cigarettes at the moment, if not much else."

He picked up a hand-rolled cigarette and placed it in front of me, smiling cheerfully as he did so. He had rather dark, sharp features, not unlike my magician uncle's. The actual structure of his face, however, was something of a puzzle for, though some aspects of it were quite impressive, others—the eyes, nose, and mouth, for example—seemed to have been stuck on as an afterthought, giving an inevitably clownish impression which made it hard to take him seriously.

"Thanks, but I don't smoke. I was wondering what that record you were just playing was."

"Debussy's *L'Après-midi d'un faune*. Do you like it?"

He then launched into an eloquent speech of about ten minutes' duration which he clearly found very entertaining. It was heavily spiced with names and quotations that were all a complete blank to me, reminding me strongly of the way my uncle had introduced obscure medical terms into his stories. I was so baffled by it all that ultimately I had to confess my ignorance in these matters.

"You've never heard of the goddess who disappeared, or of the writer from Lübeck? I don't believe it. I know all about you —you spend the whole day reading."

It was true that I did read a good deal, but mainly stories about ant men from Mars in boys' magazines, which was embarrassing to admit; but he finally accepted the fact that I was as ignorant as I claimed to be, and instead of being appalled he seemed almost to admire me for it.

"You're quite a rarity these days, you know. All the high-school students I've met so far go on talking for hours, foaming at the mouth so much you'd think they were having a fit. Still, you're not twenty yet; just give you a bit more time and you'll be babbling with the best of them. Let's just hope it's not real epilepsy."

Far from cheering me up as they were meant to do, his remarks only made me feel slightly nervous, because I'd been having blackouts occasionally since primary school. I had even been taken to a teaching hospital where they'd tried to induce a fit to see if it was epilepsy or not. The results of the test had been inconclusive, so I decided now was a good chance to get a medical opinion from this doctor-to-be, and I gave him a fairly lengthy, detailed account of my experience with the swarms of insects attracted by the veranda light and the way I had fainted afterward.

"That was an experience of Absolute Beauty," he cried when I was only halfway through my story. "What you saw then was Ideal Beauty. Beauty is a very frightening thing, you see. It's like the Gorgon, the face of Medusa. One look and you're turned into stone. Luckily beauty seldom appears in all its nakedness, and we're usually blind to it anyway, so nothing disastrous happens."

I was taken aback by this, staring at his splendidly disordered face as he went on cheerfully talking, but finally managing to slip in a question.

"Are you saying that Medusa was beautiful?"

"Who ever said anything of the sort?" he replied, assuming a provokingly nonchalant expression. "Medusa was the most hideous of the three Gorgon sisters, the most awful thing man has ever looked at, probably.... Yet it's a very odd thing that Greek mythology, normally so concerned with the human form as a whole, should have described her only in terms of her head. What, after all, was the real genesis of this monster?—bearing in mind, as we always ought to do, that myths aren't just some idle flight of fancy. What was the essential meaning of this monster that was just a head? Now there's a really interesting question for you. Some say she represents the sea, or nightmare, or the pale face of the moon. One scholar has even argued that the snakes in her hair are phallic symbols."

He gave an eccentric little laugh at this point, then returned to my first question, ignoring my obvious bewilderment. Unfortunately, when it came to the "essential meaning" of my illness, he had nothing original to say on the subject at all, though he spoke with enormous gravity.

"It certainly has some features in common with epilepsy," he concluded. "That seems undeniable. But if it isn't epilepsy, then all one can say is that it's something else."

Thinking about this later, it struck me that he not only resembled my uncle physically but was almost his double in every way. He was a magician of the intellectual kind, a man with no home to return to, a drifter on the shores of life who collected pretty shells without even getting his fingers wet, then cheerfully used them in some clever sleight of hand. And even when he said things that made a real impression on me, there was always something ridiculous about him, a trait he shared with my uncle, as if everything he did was bound to provoke the sort of wry, dismissive laughter that was heard when that other pleasantly absurd young man made his brilliant diagnosis of my kidney disease.

Yet I still looked up to him as he went on eloquently lecturing his unenlightened pupil, this time on the nature of those symptoms of mine which suggested a form of alienation from reality.

"You have headaches. You can't sleep. You have sudden fears. Your body feels out of touch with the real world, as if it were melting away. Do you realize how serious that is? If I told you it was cholera or cancer you'd be really shaken, wouldn't you? But if I told you all your troubles were psychological you'd just dismiss it as a sort of minor breakdown. What a rotten way to treat the psyche! But all modern medicine is like that. We should go back to what the ancients did, return to using spells and incantations. Modern medicine, based as it is on physiology and anatomy, should seek out its roots, the ground from which it all began. Don't you agree?"

"Yes, I really think that's true."

"True? Of course it's not. I just wanted to feel what it would be like to say that sort of thing."

"Perhaps I should just forget about it, then?"

"Well, it's not likely to get better, at least not with shock treatment or drugs. As old Philetus said, there is no other cure but that they should kiss, embrace, and lie down naked together."

"What's all that about?"

"Daphnis and Chloë's love sickness."

"Don't be silly. I'm not in ..."

"... love. That's what you were going to say, isn't it? But, even if we accept the fact that you think you aren't, people are always in love with something, you know. Now, for a start, what sort of things do you consider beautiful?"

"What do I find beautiful? Well, clouds, I suppose; insects. Then ... yes, green acorns."

"Acorns? Come on! What about people? What about girls?"

"Well, girls are beautiful, I suppose."

"You *suppose* they are? They most *certainly* are," he spluttered, spraying a certain amount of saliva about the place. "As the poet said, the body is a temple. What we call beauty is all in fact present in our sex. That might be going too far, perhaps, but are you familiar with the superb configurations of organic life? Are you aware of the amazing colors of the layers of subcutaneous fat— that bloodcurdling yellow, like dissolved quartz crystals endowed with life and decay? Of course I'm actually talking about a corpse preserved in formalin, but those wonderfully elastic white nerves, those spinal nerves; why, they're almost half an inch in diameter, and so highly strung. And the intricate structure of the vascular system: just touch it anywhere with a scalpel and the blood comes spurting out. And the rich swelling of the great muscles in the buttocks.... Well, I'm afraid I do tend to get rather carried away. Sounds like one of Hans Castorp's rhapsodies, that 'problem child of life.' But we've got to see that the body, love, and death, these three things are really one, and we ought to shout it from the rooftops...."

It was putting it lightly to say he got "carried away" at times, but all I could do was go on sitting there like an idiot with mouth agape, listening to these extraordinary remarks.

"Consider it from another point of view, then. Look at the lovely line of the collarbone and the shoulder blades, the deliciously delicate curve of the nape of the neck. Look, if I just raise my head, there's the Adam's apple here, the thyroid cartilage, and this undulating muscle here is called the... er, the ..."

"Sternocleidomastoid, I believe."

"That's right. That's right. Surprising, some of the things you seem to know." The medical student was slightly disconcerted, but soon recovered his composure, and a look of deep contemplation appeared on his face.

"People do, of course, know lots of funny things. It's only to be expected. And there's bound to be some appropriate reason for it, even if the person himself isn't aware of it. For example, if someone falls in love with a particular girl there's always—deep down—a perfectly natural motive involved. I mean, just think how some people are attracted by round faces and others by long ones. It's a very mysterious business. I prefer triangular ones myself. Always have done."

"So the fact of one's falling in love for the first time with somebody is determined by natural causes?"

"Exactly. And one has to remember that people can still fall in love even if it's not with someone of the opposite sex. Everything is determined by our infancy, by the way the scars left in our nervous system happen to affect us."

I hadn't wanted to hear the word "infancy." I found it painful, as if it had touched a thorn buried deep in me. But he changed the subject at that point, treating me to various observations on the nature of dreams. He called the dream our second life, a letter which remains unopened, a message from the world of the subconscious. I was able to join in to some extent in this talk about the mysterious, unstable nature of things encountered in one's sleep, for since that special night I'd been carefully collecting the fragments of my dreams and studying them. This, however, produced a look of even greater astonishment on his face than when I'd named that neck muscle. He stared intently at me, then said in an unnervingly gentle voice:

"You're doing well enough without reading any of those tiresome books. Still, you ought to know something about mythology, because myths make use of the same language as dreams. It's more than just the irresponsible fantasizing of primitive men. Take these myths I'm reading about at the moment, for example, from the Assam region of India. According to the Āhoms, the

Creation went like this. In the beginning nothing existed except water, and then the highest god, known as Phu-Ha-Ta-Ra, told the sky to produce light. Then, after creating his own form, he made a tortoise, a huge snake with eight heads, and finally, by degrees, the rest of the world. The forefathers of the king of the Āhoms descended from the sky and established a kingdom. It's interesting that they too have a myth about the Flood. The whole world was inundated, and only an old man called Tāholibrin escaped with one cow in a boat made of stone. Now, what do you notice about all these remote and ancient tales? You notice all sorts of similarities, almost as if there was some form of collusion. And why should that be? Because myths are all symbolic of the human soul. What we find in all myths everywhere in the world is a record of the history of the soul, of everything that has happened to it. Our longing for the past has been skillfully refined everywhere into a myth of the Golden Age. Then there's ..."

He went on and on in this way, until he either decided that the boy listening to these profundities wasn't up to understanding them, or simply ran out of steam, for he stopped to light one of his hand-rolled cigarettes and, with an expression appropriate to a budding doctor on his face, said:

"You shouldn't spend all your time shut up in your room. The weather's nice now. Why don't you go out a bit, take a walk in the country, get up into the mountains?"

"Climb a mountain? You must be joking. It's just about all I can manage to lie in bed."

This flippant reply seemed to infuriate my learned friend. His disordered face became suddenly even more distorted. He thrust out his arm, pointing to the world beyond the window, and said:

"Don't be so stupid! You're destroying yourself. Stop arguing with me and go out into the Alps and lose yourself in nature. Go on, get up those mountains!"

* * *

It must have been some days later that I went, at a time when the scents of late spring were mingling with the breath of early summer, on a bright, sunny day, a garishly bright day. I spent thirty minutes swaying about on a bus before reaching the nearest mountains, where I hadn't been for ages. The decision to go was in no way influenced by the medical student's loud advice; all I had in mind, in fact, was picking some edible bracken to add something to my meager diet. Unfortunately, a great number of people seemed to have had the same idea, and there wasn't a scrap of the stuff to be found anywhere. To make matters worse, I managed to acquire some large holes in my army boots, the only decent pair I had.

Even so, I still felt unusually cheerful and at ease with myself. On the grassy heath, white butterflies were gently fluttering their neat, almost transparent wings. They were pellucid whites, belonging to the Parnassius species (*Parnassius citrinarius*, in fact), from the home of Apollo and the Muses. In Germany this butterfly (or at least one that closely resembles it) is called the *Apollo Falter*, and its pure white wings have a red-veined pattern on them with a tinge of blackwood green. But, though the *Apollo Falter* isn't to be seen here in Japan, the local variety—the only example of its type—makes up for this by an immaculate elegance which its more exotic-looking counterpart lacks.

One of these pellucid whites flew in front of me as if showing me which way to take. The path dipped and turned, but the butterfly kept floating on before me and urging me to go with her.

The word "floating" is the right one, for her light frame seemed suspended in the air, borne along only slightly by the almost nonexistent breeze, and she had such a casual attitude to life that inwardly I couldn't help telling her to be more careful, advising her that I might look harmless enough now but in my day I had slaughtered any number of her friends.

This lighthearted warning of mine was very shortly borne out by actual events, for a small boy suddenly leaped out from behind a bush with a net in his hand (and a triangular canister strapped to his waist, which I spotted immediately), and took a swipe at the butterfly. Luckily the first lunge of the dreaded net was slightly off target, so she just managed to slip under it and, despite her natural sedateness, showed she had a considerable turn of speed once startled out of her complacency. But she must have been more than startled, was probably in a panic, since she merely flew around in circles in her efforts to escape. Her pursuer was also overexcited, revealing his inexperience by making two or three more swishes at her which again, miraculously, she managed to evade. This, by now, was more than I could bear to watch; and, with the old spirit surging up in me, I ran over to the boy, grabbed his net, and made a gentle pass with it one-handed. The butterfly was just about to rise higher up, and landed neatly in the mesh.

I carefully disentangled her wings so as not to damage them, then, still holding her captive, turned toward the boy. He must have been around eleven or so, and looked rather neat and trim compared to most of the local children. He seemed quite stunned by the whole episode, though his innocent, bright eyes showed obvious signs of admiration, too.

"Thanks very much," he said, nervously accepting the butterfly I handed him, and putting her away inside the container lined with oilpaper. He didn't seem to have much else in there.

"What else have you caught?" I asked. He looked up at me, hesitated briefly, then seemed to make up his mind and told me in a slightly incoherent mumble that he'd got a Libytheidae and an alpine brown skipper.

I understood his hesitation for, after all, what was the point of mentioning these elaborate names to people who weren't interested and knew nothing about them? All you could hope for was at most a dubious silence, or a rather irritating pretense of curiosity. I'd had the experience a number of times myself, and knew how unpleasant it was. What's a Libytheidae? Let's have a look. Oh, it's just an ordinary old butterfly. And the precious object would get all the scales rubbed off its wings in the process. So, in order to lull these suspicions, I said quite casually:

"What about small Gifu butterflies? I should have thought there'd be lots around here."

It was a pleasure to see his face immediately light up.

"Small Gifu butterflies? The standard ones as well?"

"Yes, but their distribution tends to be limited to particular parts of this region, and as far as I remember you'll only find the small variety here.... How long have you been collecting? Only butterflies, or other things?"

"This is my third year. I've started collecting beetles, too, this year, but I don't know the names very well yet.... I like shadow-hand butterflies best."

"Shadow-hand ... shadow-hand." I muttered the unfamiliar name to myself. "Ah, you mean what we used to call the zephyrus."

But he'd never heard of a zephyrus; the name belonged to a generation before his. It applied to a number of small gray butterflies with a thin tail-shaped projection on their hind wings which made them look like tiny angels, and it had sentimental associations for any of the old school of butterfly collectors. There had even been a magazine named after it. Anyone could work out from that how long ago it was that I'd actually been wielding a butterfly net.

Since my middle-school years I'd felt a particular attraction toward this part of the world, and my close acquaintance with collectors' records and local catalogues stood me in good stead now. While I was binding the damaged soles of my boots with some string I'd brought with me, I told the boy about the kind of zephyrus butterflies you could find in this area. He then drew out of his pocket a small box with insects in it, and I told him the name of each one as he asked me them.

"But this one's not in the book," he said.

"I'm not surprised. Those books are fine for butterflies and cicadas, but you get to hymenoptera and there are kinds even specialists don't know about."

"In that case I'll really start collecting insects properly. It sounds much more fun. I bet I'll discover a new species."

He had got over his initial shyness with a stranger, and his eyes shone, reminding me of all that I'd experienced at his age: the wonder on being allowed to look into my magician uncle's microscope; the time when I finally made up my mind to send off a specimen to a specialist, and the joy I'd felt on receiving confirmation that this was a species which hadn't been spotted for years. All of this was expressed in his tiny face, along with a child's respect for a grown-up who shared the same interest and knew so much more. It wasn't a particularly good-looking face, but there was something about it I found touching, perhaps because it reminded me a little of the boy staggering under the weight of his army rifle, the girl in khaki overalls working away with her file, or the other girl in school uniform looking up at the approaching bus.

"Are you here by yourself?"

"No, my sister's with me. She got tired and went to lie down in the grass. She ought to be here soon."

"Do you live around here?"

"No. We're just visiting relations in Matsumoto. We've got to go back tomorrow. You wouldn't like to go with me to the meadows, would you? It would be super if we could go together."

He spoke for the first time in a genuinely childish voice, and looked up at me with a pleading expression on his face. If he had been alone I would probably have suggested the same thing myself, but at the bend in the path below us a girl had just appeared, her head wrapped in what looked like a large handkerchief, and casually dressed in trousers and tennis shoes. It was clear at a glance that the girl was his elder sister, not so much because he smiled at her in recognition but from some basic similarity in their features, although hers were much more delicately formed. It was the kind of similarity that ladybirds have despite the myriad variations in the patterns of their spots.

She must have been a year or two older than me, though the symmetry of her features, together with her slightly suspicious expression, made her look probably more grown-up than she was. After calling out her brother's name, she stood there swinging a light-looking valise in her hand, then started moving slowly in our direction with her head downcast. But from the very first moment I felt uneasy, knowing somehow in advance that her effect on me would be far stronger than her younger brother's charm. The emotions I'd felt in the past were coming to life again, for I had already noticed the slender neck, the black eyes,

128

the auburn-tinted hair showing beneath her scarf; and my growing sense of panic made it impossible for me to stay.

"Right. I'll be off, then," I said, and stood up.

"But I thought we were going to the meadows."

I gave a very firm shake of my head, and pointed to the right.
The path conveniently divided into two just there, the right fork
descending through thick shrub toward the gorge below. I set off
walking and heard the boy call out goodbye in a regretful tone of
voice, so I looked back for a moment, and my eyes and his sister's
met. She had just reached him, and seemed to be smiling slightly,
a puzzled smile, though it reminded me of the ambiguous smile
that conjurers often have. I wasn't sure what to do, so I bowed
slightly in her direction. Why did I have to do something fatuous
like that? What did I think I was up to? Feeling embarrassed
and annoyed with myself I made off at a great pace, plunging
into the vegetation and forcing my way through. I tore off leaves
from the bushes that overhung the path, kicked aside or leaped
over any branches that got in my way, not so much walking as
running. The path led down to the gorge, and there it petered
out.

The smell of damp foliage, of rotting leaves accumulated at
the water's edge, greeted my arrival. A clear mountain stream
flowed furiously by, shaking the ferns whose leaves trailed in the
water. The broad-leaved trees kept off the rays of the sun, letting
the light through only in places, and that thin light itself seemed
to be absorbed by the humus on the banks. I sat down on a rock
and watched the endless swirling of the current, listening to a
rhythmic murmur which seemed to permeate it all. For a long
while I was troubled by some inner turmoil I didn't fully understand, and yet I made no attempt to seek its cause. What I
needed now was only quiet, soft indolence; and this I found, for

with a rock as my pillow and lulled by the constant sound of flowing water I drifted off to sleep.

I must have slept for a little under an hour, but even then I remained in a sort of drowsy, melancholic trance, and lay there thinking vaguely about things, sometimes watching the movements of the birds singing overhead. An image gradually formed in my mind, the face of a girl who had once appeared in a dream; but time past and present played tricks with it, and elements of another face—of the girl I had just met—attached themselves to it. All our images from the past are composite and unreliable, even at times complete fictions occasioned by some face only existing in the present; but I was still too confused to work out the truth of this, and gave in to a mild self-pity instead, a longing, for example, for the warmth of an ordinary home. The melody of that flute came back to me, and I whistled it aloud, the gradual rise and then the trembling fall. The sound of the reed pipe, the syrinx, was more than I could manage, yet the notes had their own slender beauty as they scattered into the sky's deep blue, through which the sun maintained its measured voyage. I noticed that my eyes seemed to be full of tears. I stood up and washed my face in the cold mountain stream, not knowing which were tears and which were drops of water.

As evening approached I walked up the gentle slope from the grassy plateau toward the top of the mountain, waving a meager bunch of withered bracken in my hand. The mountain was called Ōgabana, the King's Nose, and seen from the plain of Matsumoto it was a conspicuous outcrop of rock, whereas from the plateau of Utsukushigahara it was little more than a protuberance on the edge of it. For me, however, it was a place of memories, the mountain I had climbed on first coming to this region. The peak—a peak only in name for it was just a cramped space made higher than the rest by a pile of slate-like rocks—still had the same stone images arranged on it, and I felt a pang of genuine nostalgia. What had changed was the season, much earlier in the year now than then, and the great, ranged waves of the far Alps to the west were still draped in the cloak of winter. On the high places and in the folds between them the winter snow remained clearly visible even behind a veil of mist, and in the valleys flowed what looked like clouds of steam, impossible to distinguish as the fog of winter or the haze of spring, and probably a mixture of the two.

The western side of the mountain fell away quite steeply, with clusters of bushes and various small trees wandering down to the flat area below. When I'd first come here, that was the way I had ascended, and I could see the faint outline of a path crossing the grassy upland before disappearing into the bushes; and just at the point where it did so there were two lone figures in white. My first thought was that it must be the brother and sister, but they could hardly still be wandering about here as late as this, so I quickly decided it was someone else. As I looked around me, however, I felt flustered and confused again, then sat down on a lichen-covered rock and listened to the beating of my pulse, listened attentively for a while, anxiously, as though threatened by something that remained unknown....

This restless, muddled state, experienced at an age when age itself still seems unreal, is either acknowledged as love, a fitting object for our earnest and admiring gaze, or else dismissed as something rather crude and nasty, and preferably ignored; as if discriminating in this simpleminded way could protect us from the complications of real life. I had more or less adopted the latter attitude at the time, that it was a simple matter of sexual desire—even if the simple matter itself was one I knew little about—and that I should try to suppress these dangerous feelings. I decided it was something the passage of the years finally aroused in late boyhood, yet it was still close to a child's passion for certain toys. My two or three earlier experiences had been like that, and since they'd been lacking in any conscious sense of sexual longing, I assumed my feelings now shared the same kind of innocence....

One day when I was working in the factory, the rumble of the machines was pierced by a high-pitched scream. One of the girl workers had got her fingers caught in the bite of a milling tool. Those nearest all swarmed about her, and from behind that human wall I saw some people picking up the girl, who had fainted. The belt had been switched off immediately, and just the head of the machine was swaying gently as if perplexed. Her sleeve guards were soaked with lubricating oil, and as they were rolled up I was struck by the unexpected whiteness of her skin, and by the strange attraction of the bright red liquid dripping down it, tracing lines along her arm. I knew it was just blood, but the color was beautiful, making such a strong impression on me that I felt a slight stifling sensation in my chest.

This was something I'd experienced several times before, a sensation so slight one wasn't quite sure it had ever existed; and the last of those occasions I recalled came from the distant past. It was a rather childish episode, perhaps, but for me it contained the essence, the real heart of what such experiences were all about.

We often stayed at a house at the foot of a mountain when I was small, and though the summit was no more than three thousand feet above sea level, I never dreamed of climbing it. Wherever I looked the mountain was covered with thick, dark green forests, or with grassy slopes and red-brown cliffs. But when I was in my first year at middle school and my passion for collecting insects had just started, I began to wonder what kind of fabulous insects there might be on that mountaintop. I only had to think about it and the peak became a sacred place, a place of mystery that made my heart beat fast.

One morning, without telling anybody, I set off alone up the narrow mountain path. I imagine the feelings of a man seeking some legendary land beyond the setting sun or a mountaineer starting the ascent of some still unconquered Himalayan peak must be very similar to those I experienced then. On I went, my thoughts fixed only on reaching the top, so obsessed with it I didn't once look around at the world gradually opening out below me, urging on my tired legs with that one aim in mind. The path stretched endlessly upward, and the sweat flowed, dried out, then flowed again, and the peak must have been getting nearer but there was never any sign of it. At every bend on the way I was sure I would see it this time, but the path zigzagged on, growing steeper, narrower, and that was all.

Finally I arrived at what seemed to be the top, though it had little to show for it. There were just a few bushes and ancient trees twisted by the wind, and no view whatsoever since it was all hidden behind the vegetation. It had to be the top, however, because the path started to slope down a little way off, and there was a stone with some faded inscription on it.

Feeling dazed and worn out, I sat down on the root of a tree. From time to time, a breeze came and cooled my body. I looked up at the sunlight directly overhead, then, almost reeling from its glare, turned my eyes away toward the trunk of the dead tree, grotesquely split by lightning and smothered in something whitish gray. Lichen had eaten away its bark and ivy snaked about its branches, dangling down from them in several places. I looked at all this, and as I looked I felt a faint, mysterious shuddering in my arms and legs, as though some pagan spirit had occupied the air around me, something as palpable and real as the sharp odor of the rank vegetation. The leaves drank in the sunlight, eagerly, insatiably, breathing with quiet, almost painful sighs. I could just make out the buzzing of two-winged flies, borne to me on the limpid air; then noticed them hovering here and there in spaces free of vegetation. And I, too, breathed in this vast, unseen, and awe-inspiring air which nature breathes, filling every corner of this mountaintop.

I sat quite still for a while, and suddenly I felt the sheer extent of the mountain on which I was casually sitting with outstretched legs, the richness of the foliage covering its sides, the far depths of the sky above it; confirming—as I now understand, years later—a sense of my own essential solitude. A surge of weary, sad, and empty feelings, a kind I'd rarely come across before, swept through me. Then, from deep inside my body an ominous, unknown force seemed to rise in me, and I threw myself face down on the grass. And so, under a downpour of high summer light, in the stifling odor of the plants, to the erotic buzzing of the gadflies' wings, and savoring the endless warmth and comfort of the earth, I had my very first emission.

I suppose people will probably laugh if I say that the object of my desire was nature itself.

... Twilight was falling. Shadows were filling the pure pale blue of the sky. A cold air, cold as that at dusk in early spring, gradually descended.

The sun withdrew its beams, drawn into the rich folds of the valleys to my left. The sense of distance faded from the far-off peaks, and they seemed near, only two-dimensional now, fantastic forms deprived of their usual severity. Then they became at last a mass of deep purple shadow, starkly revealed in the dying light. I had already forgotten what that girl looked like, her image driven from my mind by the scene spread out before me, for in the deep peace of these undulations and convergences, all the sinking away from me of the enormous earth, I felt I heard the spirit of the mountains calling out to me. And my innocent body trembled in recollection, shook at the overpowering desire aroused in me, the desire for what was past and present and to come; and in my heart were recognitions made and vows, knowing as I did that the place from which I'd come was nothing but the natural world, and nature thus to me would always be the source of my truest being, a perfect relationship never to be forgotten.

4

From then on the natural world became a living part of my environment—nature in all its aspects: as something cold in its rejection, or warmly to be loved; silent and unmoving, or whispering in special words; a source of restful sleep, or of awakening desire—all this felt vividly, on the skin, as if I'd finally arrived on holy ground, a place where all that had been passed down through generations from the farthest corners of the earth could now at last be handed on to me, the opening out before me of the world.

This, specifically, applied to what lay quite close at hand: the Japan Alps, range after range of peaks pointing to heaven, vigorous, sensitive, beautiful, rough-hewn yet with all the signs of careful workmanship. I had a plan—it seems reckless now, the sort of thing that only a young man convinced he could do anything on his own would undertake. But, as far as my resources would allow, which meant the amount of food I could scrape together, I decided to explore those mountains, to climb the steep gullies, traverse the ridges. So with no fixed daily schedule I slid down rock faces with the aid of a length of discarded rope, and spent nights in the shadow of some boulder, wrapped in a sleeping bag borrowed from the school mountaineering club; then drove my feeble body on in a kind of mindless rage as I climbed from one cold, gray, jutting rock to the next. Once, I fell off, a drop of about ten feet, but I managed to get away with only a few cuts and nothing broken. Another time I was caught on a ridge in a violent downpour accompanied by claps of thunder, and was chilled to the bone. When I finally managed to reach a mountain hut there was no bedding of any kind, since it wasn't the official season; so I spent the whole night trying not to freeze to death. I suppose I must have looked like a wild animal in the grip of some obscure compulsion to keep moving on.

Still, on most days nature looked kindly on me. The crowds of stars seen at midnight from a mountain peak were like nothing one could imagine in this world, and when I stood bathed in light from the sky's enormous, deep blue dome, with the twisted lines of the snow-filled gullies casting back that light, and looked far down on a valley where the new leaves had at last come out, I was bound to feel the privilege of standing on a mountaintop under such a sky. The air on the peaks had its own peculiar clarity which, once breathed, made one forget the impurities of the lower world, as if some constant renewal of the heart took place in that unending silence, something felt in one's blood but not to be expressed in words.

At moments like these I felt that the hidden things I sought might even now reveal themselves, seeing a premonition in the form of some lichen-covered rock, or in the windings of the branches of the creeping pine, the glittering of water flowing under fallen leaves; just as, in the past, I had waited in the hope that something might appear in the huge mirror at home.

Something should be said about the seasonal changes in this region. The air in winter is bitterly cold, actually hurting one's bare skin. The mountains soar up high, with a unique sense of weight in their rise and fall; sometimes a range of black shapes with a mere scattering of snow on them, sometimes white peaks blindingly reflecting the sun's rays. Blends of the most subtle shades occasionally appear, then bursts of pure light to dazzle the eyes.

Spring comes, the snow melts on the banks of streams, and with the sound of it falling into the water below, one looks out toward the distant Alps to find their shapes all floating now behind a finespun haze. Clouds of a thicker mist drift along the valleys, and in the hollows the fuchsia's delicate flowers are already in bloom. But in the mountains spring is inevitably late, and when the upper snows have finally melted every valley is filled with the roar of floodwater, turbid, thudding against the banks which collapse in places, while paths are destroyed as trees borne down by the current are cast up and left lying across them. Eventually most of this destruction disappears, being merely one sign of the quickening of the earth repeated every year. The more remote parts of the Alps may still show here and there these scenes of violence, but in the foothills and meadows to the east the rich rebirth of spring can be seen spreading swiftly upward. The round buds of the larches swell with each fall of rain, and the cuckoo returns, filling the woods and forests with its simple, plaintive call. And when the grass fattens on the uplands and the azalea buds show signs of opening, then already the soft winds of early summer will be swaying the branches of the trees.

I spent a number of such days lying in a wood, listening for hours to the rustling of the new leaves. In my hands would be an open book, but I read almost nothing, a few lines being enough either to occupy my mind or to induce the heavy sleep that eluded me at night. Sometimes I had shallow, seemingly reluctant dreams, which vanished almost as soon as they had come. I remember one occasion when the wind rose, fluttering first one leaf and then another, spreading from branch to branch, and my eyes half opened as I seemed to hear a faint music in the sound, again the melancholy solo of a flute, its rise and inconsolable fall. This stimulated another, visual illusion, not sufficient to be called a dream, where far off in the shadow of the bushes lay a faun who raised his body to a sitting position and placed a reed pipe to his lips. This wasn't the satyr figure pictured in mythology, a hideous, hairy creature, but one with a slim body and dappled skin, probably based on a photo of Nijinsky in that role which the medical student had shown me. Then yet another image came to me, a more daring one, of a naked nymph with wanton hair seen intermittently in the blue shade of the forest depths. (Years later I saw Serge Lifar dance the main role in this ballet, and yet, as far as I'm concerned, my own naïve though very detailed fantasy outshone his stage performance.) But just as the nymph bent her white body backward the whole illusion vanished. I looked up at the sky between the branches, enjoying the feeling of the grass underneath my back. A pine needle fell, softly pricking my cheek....

The real vitality of spring reaches the western mountains round about this time. On the high plateau, birds in great numbers suddenly appear, and amid their constant whistling the bushes start to unfurl their reddish-tinged leaves. In places where lately the snow remained, in the still damp shadows of trees overhung by cliffs, green plants emerge, soon covering the earth. Here and there at the side of the road small flowers have spread a cloth of stippled white, but if one climbs further up, the paths through the forests are still indistinguishable in the snow, which has only melted in a fringe of small holes around the trees. Finally one reaches the region of creeping pines, and here there is no snow, although in the withered grass on the slopes there is the occasional ribbon of it, from the base of which water drips slowly down. But even in this scene of apparent desolation and decay, if one looks closely, one can find not only traces of green but a fair number of shortia plants just starting to bud. Once the long winter is over, the transition from spring to summer here is almost immediate, and within less than a fortnight these slopes will be covered with the broad petals of globeflowers, a sea of yellow flooding the whole surface, a transformation with the speed and brilliance of magic. There are countless varieties of flowers in these high places: the dicentra which blooms in groups in stony ground; the black fritillaria appearing singly with its elegant, dark purple flower in unexpected spots; flowers like stars, like bells, or of various indeterminate shapes, vying in the vividness of their colors to induce the insects to visit them; forms of organic life in every one of which appears a miracle of natural design, of intricate patterning.

But what of those flowers that fly, the butterflies of the high mountains? There is a fairly plain-looking one, distinguished from others of the grayling species by the yellow-brown crest on its wings, called the reddish satyrid or *Erebia ligea takanonis*, which drifts leisurely around among the various flowers, then seems to fall into that multicolored sea. In contrast to it, the smaller fritillary flies at great speed through the upper air, rests briefly on some rock where it flexes its wings a few times, and then is off like lightning again. The alpine spotted yellow, with a thick black belt conspicuous on her yellow dress, wanders among the bilberry bushes until she finds a leaf to her liking on which, arching her abdomen, she lays her pure white eggs. Then there is the *Anthocaris cardamine*, small angel wings balancing its white body so gracefully that it seems like the spirit of the wind, glittering in the rose-colored light of early morning, and only ever seen by the occasional mountaineer.... All these appeared before me as I lay there half asleep—dancing in the breeze or poised on flowers, displaying their finery. This was the first time I had actually seen any of them alive, but I felt no urge to catch them. It is one of the more unpleasant aspects of the collector, as even a man like Hudson has admitted, that the most beautiful of butterflies, should it belong to an ordinary species, will merely look ordinary in his eyes. But I was looking with the eyes of infancy again, and was totally absorbed in the sight, wondering at the strange chain of circumstances that had resulted in the eddying colors and singular patterns on their wings; and I smiled to myself, both for their sake and my own....

As I watched the subtle movements of those rainbow wings, I was reminded of the happiest moments of my childhood when, crude net in hand, I spent endless days amid the rich scent of summer grass, under the burning eye of the sun, in eager pursuit of others of their kind. All that forgotten excitement welled up again in me, like a beam of light flooding the mind. I wondered whether these might not be the last spirits of nature, all that remained of the departed wood nymphs, so hazardous were their lives, so silently, transiently alight in the air around me. I under-

141

stood why the ancients had readily linked them with the concept of the soul, which is why, perhaps, I have told a similar tale, similar in its simplicity and its symbolic implications, traveling the same path as all those primitive, unenlightened people who were astonished by the appearances of things.

Another butterfly—a peacock—landed in front of me, wrapped in brilliant light, with that wonderful eye pattern on its four wings. Its Latin name is *Vanessa io*, Io being the daughter of the king of Argos, beloved of Jove, who turned her into a white heifer to protect her from the jealousy of Hera; but Hera tormented her with a gadfly which drove her across the various countries of Europe and through Asia. One morning as the sun rose in a foreign land and the tired girl woke up, a newborn butterfly flew up from where she lay; the girl's tears had fallen on its wings, and, ever since, the peacock butterfly has borne the sad relic of those tears, still shining there like pearls. Legend has also been preserved in the name of a woodland herb with four ovate leaves, called truelove or *Paris quadrifolia* after the warrior who awarded the golden apple to Aphrodite in return for Helen, and was the cause of the long Trojan war. Similarly, the modest, drooping flower of the *Leucothoe keiskei* is said to represent the white neck of Leucothoe, whom the Sun God loved. The *Cassiope lycopodiodes*, which clusters in stony ground on mountain ridges, and the *Andromeda pollifolia* with its small pot-shaped flowers, both bear the names of mythical figures immortalized in two adjacent constellations, although on summer nights it is probably the Swan and the Archer that much more readily bring to mind the old Greek myths.

Once, looking up at a shower of distant specks of light in a wonderfully clear sky, I thought for a moment that I might become what people call a poet, something I'd never dreamed of being before. It was like that time when I'd been drawing with pastels at school and felt some other person's energy buried in me and beginning to emerge; and, as though a longing for some elusive prospect of this kind could somehow physically be caught and held, I reached out for it with both hands. But the poet in me refused to speak: what I wanted to express remained just a movement in my throat, a trembling in my lips. I felt an eddy of emotion break inside me, but it soon subsided, then withdrew and vanished, leaving nothing but a sense of emptiness.

I was ashamed of indulging in this fantasy, telling myself that almost anybody would be moved by some such feelings under a sky like that, and would suffer similar illusions of self-importance. But then, a little later, I began to think that perhaps a time might come when my eyes would open, when I would be able to see through outward appearances to the heart of things. Yet this thought, too, only made me frown in disbelief, and, dismissing it with a shrug of my shoulders, I took my mess tin out of my rucksack, opened it, and extracted a piece of bread which I stuffed into my mouth, wondering if poets were as greedy as I seemed to be.

The emotions aroused by the mountains are not always generous ones, nor do they usually last very long, being as changeable as the weather. In this instance, I found myself giving in first to irritation, feeling some unspecified need, and then to physical desires provoked by equally unknown causes. Waves of lust swept through me, followed by a desperate sense of solitude. Abruptly, I raised my head and, under a parched sky, looked at the scene around me in all its symmetry. Everything was clean, everything quite frigid and empty of emotion, the natural world of order, uniformity, and perfect balance. I tore up a clump of grass and rubbed my face in the black earth underneath. I hungered for the smell of the beast; I longed to be pure animal, to be other than myself. I even prayed that a clap of thunder might destroy me; or, in its stead, that I should find the bird of thunder, a snow grouse on its nest, and strangle all its young. I rolled down the steep slope. As I rolled, I hated the plants I touched, their thorns, their smell. I went on rolling madly in this way until I was stopped by a large bush, cutting my hand on one of its branches. I made no effort to stand up, but lay there for a long time licking my hand like a wounded animal.

Eventually autumn comes, its peaceful days a sign that soon it will be time for withering and decay, for the earth to freeze over. The birch leaves turn completely yellow; one leaf falls from the very tip of a branch, and, before long, the whole valley is strewn with them. The wind blows; the leaves are caught up in it, wafted and drifting in a sky now hard and deeply blue. Already the bright fields of flowers have been laid bare, ravaged now and darkened by the frosts. All flows in the reverse direction to spring, the solemn shadows of decline moving down the mountainsides. In the foothills there are still clusters of tall grass and trees, in yellows, reds, dark browns, receiving the soft rays of the sun like a string of beads, glowing in the last of the light; while on the forest roads the scattered needles of the larches are raked into pale brown lines by an overnight fall of rain.

Most telling of these signs of sad departure, however, is the new purity of the Azusakawa, the Catalpa River, giving the cold, clear impression that some other force of nature is waiting nearby to approach. And, sure enough, it soon does, for one morning your eyes open to see on the farthest peaks, on that huge range of light brown rocks, still faint yet unmistakable, the footprints the snow queen has left behind her after her nocturnal dance. Within a few days, while the weakening sun is still shining on the faded autumn leaves, you notice traces of white around the mountain hut. It is the first snow, forerunner of that snow which will cover everything over in its deep blanket. Then finally all will fall asleep in the white and terrible cold.

* * *

So far I have recorded various reminiscences, drawn from different layers of my memory. With even the most childish and naïve of memories, however, there is a maturing process, an inevitable growing with the years, just as a tree accumulates annual rings. The self that appears in memory, even though undoubtedly a child, is still just as certainly the person one is now. But there are also memories that lie completely buried, and these remain uninfluenced by time, as if time stagnated at the deepest level of one's being, or simply turned in circles there. Perhaps it is only when such buried things are suddenly exposed that a person first becomes aware of the real nature of time, can see himself as something existing in its flow, conscious of the circumstances that have formed him, not as he usually thinks of them, but as things with roots in a deeper, more distant world.

I want to write here about one or two other incidents, the specific moments when parts of my early childhood came back to life, but I have no confidence in being able to convey them properly. If the central meaning of what I relate is not transmitted but becomes a mere recital of events, then this is going to make fairly pointless reading. The truth is that every human life is a story, one into which we are born, the main theme of our being. The events we experience as having the full weight of meaning are ones that link up with this story, ones that have a primal con-

145

nection with a narrative shape already there inside us. All that we undergo, even the most trivial episode, acquires significance from that source, and things truly accidental are much rarer than people seem to think.

It was only an ordinary road through an ordinary valley. The valley gradually narrowed, and far off from a prominent cliff the mountain streams dropped down in a series of small falls to form a swirling torrent. The valley sometimes divided, and in places I had to cross dangerous-looking suspension bridges, but on the whole I managed to keep pace with the constant rhythm of the river and covered a good deal of ground. Inside, however, I felt ill at ease, some corner of me always being prone to vague unrest and introspection, though it seldom broke through my surface calm. I noticed to one side the opening of another valley, with a large waterfall in the distance; and for no reason I could understand, as it seemed just another curtain of falling water half-hidden behind trees, I was strongly drawn toward it.

But I have already taken the story too far, and must go back and describe various scenes I had encountered earlier on the road. The route was new to me, for the way in was partly concealed by fields where horseradish was being grown. The flat area that the valley joined was covered in these green plants, which were fenced off from the road by rickety posts with wire stretched between them, and, resting my hand on the wobbly fence, I stayed awhile gazing at the clumps of ovate leaves. I walked on for quite a long time, then lit a small fire between some rocks in a place which seemed far enough away from any houses, and, regardless of the hour, boiled up about half a pint of rice, sprinkled some dried miso on top, and ate it slowly. The fire was still burning, so I sat there watching the thin flames flickering in the glare of the noonday sun, until they finally went out. I then set off again, and came across a sight which took me by surprise, so familiar did it seem.

There was a glade full of whitish moths, drifting like a storm of petals or confetti in the air. They were daylight moths, of a kind I remembered well, the yellow-legged tussock variety, and they had just grown their wings, ascending and descending gently, circling the glade. It was the first time I had seen them since leaving Tokyo, but they were no different from those I'd found in my uncle's back garden as a child, particularly on that day when my sister lay waiting for death to take her away. Now, as then, they kept revisiting the home they'd come from, an old, pockmarked dogwood tree, and when I stretched out my hand to touch the coarse bark there were some of the discarded husks still attached to it, and the beads of blackish eggs in places. Everything was exactly as it had been; I had even placed my hand on the tree in the same way when I was small. I looked up at the leaves, now mere skeletons of veins, having been stripped bare by the hungry larvae, and I was filled with feelings of sadness and longing I could give no name or object to. And when I moved on up the narrowing road, I had the impression I was being drawn back into the very distant past, a feeling that lingered in me.

But to return to the present: as soon as I saw that waterfall in the distance, I somehow felt in thrall to it, knowing I had to approach it. There was no path of any kind, so I had to struggle across the damp rocks, gripping hold of creepers that hung down the cliff. I gradually got nearer until at last I could feel the cool spray blowing on my face. Drenched ferns, the tips of their leaves trembling, were at my feet, but further than this I couldn't go, for the rocks were too slippery and steep. I stood with one hand holding the edge of a rock for some time, uncertain what to do. Then, all of a sudden, a dazzling object danced before my eyes and sped away. A shudder passed along my spine, and I felt my whole body go tense as I watched, spellbound, those silver-white wings. It was a silver-underside lycaenid, I knew it right away, and the glitter came from the dust of its scales which, once before, had worked its fascination on me. And then, in the very next moment, I remembered it all, that vanished day of long ago.

Just in front of me I can see someone's back, slightly stooped and swaying, wearing a dark gray suit. I am quite sure that it's my father. Mother is also there. I can't see her face, as she appears to be listening to the guide's explanation, standing in a graceful pose. My elder sister seems to be afraid of the torrent plunging into the basin below, and is holding my hand firmly in hers. Tiny drops of water drift upward in a white mist, and I can hear a dull roar coming from the rocks we're standing on.

Then I remember a conversation. My sister is telling the legend of the waterfall, wriggling about as she does so. "Well, once there was a ..." "A woodcutter," says my mother helpfully. "There was a woodcutter. And then he got his foot caught in a spider's web. And the spider was a something sort of spider. What kind of spider was it, now?..."

My sister lived now, in my mind, just as she had been when alive: beautiful, delicate, like a perfect work of hand-carved art. There were a host of other things as well: the white folds of the mosquito net and the feeling of being at the bottom of the sea; the night visitors that came and clung to the net, fluttering their wings. I also seemed to hear quite plainly my mother and sister breathing lightly as they slept, the sound of my father turning the pages of his book.

A storm broke in my breast; my knees trembled. I found myself leaning forward to rub my face against the cold, wet rock, as though intoxicated. I did this for a while. When at last I raised my head, I saw the scenery around me with different eyes. The world of infancy had returned, confirming that for all those years I'd merely grown physically, grown tall and thin. The outer world seemed changed in almost every detail, the inner equally transformed. It was like that day when, having been confined to bed for months with a kidney infection, I was allowed outside for the very first time, and I discovered a whole new realm of sensations. It was on a day in early spring, and when I stepped down from the veranda onto the still frost-furrowed earth the dampness of it spread up through the geta I was wearing on my bare feet. Like an infant who has just learned to walk I stumbled awkwardly about, breathing in the light air through my nose. The world about me was all incomparably new, was deep, was wide, and there seemed no end to it.

What was different this time, however, was that I could physically experience the feelings of my infancy in perfect clarity, that profound, moist world of pure sensation, a twilight world made up of various layers of shadow; and in that world I experienced myself, small, timid, yet with my eyes intensely open. As each cool gust reached me from the waterfall I sensed once more the return of what had been forgotten; and I wondered that people should have the capacity to forget, to forget things that were so important to them.

At my side the wet ferns moved in the spray, great clumps of them moving only their delicate fingertips, and as they did so I saw the greenness melt from them, sliding down into the waterfall below.

One more story, this time from school, from the bookracks of the library. On the day in question I happened to ask the German teacher, whom I hardly knew, for permission to borrow a certain book. If the old high-school system had any failing in particular, I suppose it was a tendency to be indulgent toward rather dubious students who didn't turn up very often in class, and this teacher only needed one look at my dozy face to give me his consent, even taking me along to the library himself. We went through the library office, then up the stairs to the bookracks, entering by a heavy door which made a dull, creaking sound when opened. We passed through two rooms crowded with books, and I felt myself enclosed in cold, stale air, the smell of dust and mildew filling my nostrils; and this brought back to me a room in my uncle's house which no longer existed at that time. It was an old Western-style room used solely for storing things, piled high with the books my father had left us, as well as huge cabin trunks with every inch of space covered in labels, boxes containing picture scrolls, some oblong chests, and dozens of my specimen cases, too. Since the curtains were always drawn, only a very faint light crept in through the windows, revealing the layer of dust covering the various objects and the cobwebs hanging from the ceiling. For some reason I spent a lot of time in that quiet, depressing atmosphere, taking down the heavy, dark brown specimen cases and looking, perhaps, at some of my prize collection of cockchafers, shining blue and green like jewels. This anthracophora reminded me of the helmet and armor a medieval knight wore; that trichius was like a royal crest from ancient times. Or I might look at my father's solemn, old possessions, of total irrelevance to a child, which my uncle assured me would all be mine when I grew up. Sometimes I would pick up a volume of paintings, gazing at an ancient bust of a priest's head or a detailed landscape by one of the Renaissance masters. The damp pages made a faint sound as I turned them over. Or I might open one of the trunks and find an old passport issued by the Government of the Greater Japanese Empire, or German marks with a series of noughts on them, scores of foreign picture postcards, and used theater tickets. All stank of mildew, but I would scrutinize them carefully, feeling a sense of restfulness, of nostalgia in their company ... with my back slightly bowed, head tilted a little to the left, for hours on end....

"This is the shelf."

The teacher's voice interrupted these reflections—a diffident voice, yet quite piercing all the same. I looked at the row of books in front of me, in a variety of bindings with different lettering on their spines, but all by authors whose names I knew well. There, at about chest level, was the series I was looking for, in light brown cloth bindings with the titles in gold. I felt a childish excitement for a moment, much like the thrill I'd had when first getting an encyclopedia of insects, or when receiving the journal of an entomological society I'd joined much later on, which had words in a foreign language I couldn't read just below its title.

"*Joseph* doesn't seem to be here. Someone must have taken it out," the teacher said. "Well, choose anything you'd like to read. I've got to go and look for something."

He then did just that, and once his footsteps had ceased to sound on the creaking floor the room somehow felt much larger.

About two or three months before this, I happened to attend a meeting of the German Society organized by some of the students. When I looked at the printed handout we were given, I knew that my linguistic skills weren't going to be of any use with this, and since the whole thing seemed little more than an extension of what went on in class I decided to escape at the earliest convenient moment. Even so, the first line on that piece of paper caught my attention: "The well of the past is deep," this being in fact the opening line of the Prologue, "Descent into Hell," to that huge epic, massive as a pyramid, which the writer from Lübeck took sixteen years to put together.* Of course I knew absolutely nothing about this at the time, but the line still interested me enough for me to listen closely for a while to the translation provided by the teacher. I then felt sleepy and half dozed off with my head resting on the desk, but part of my mind continued to take in the general comments on the work the teacher made during a pause in his translation. His was the same oddly restrained yet piercing voice I was to hear later among the bookracks, and it reminded me then of the voice of the guide explaining the legend of the waterfall, although the story this man was describing was much older, much stranger, much richer in its symbolic implications. It was a parable of the Oriental epistemology of the Creation, of traditional Hebraic wisdom concerning primitive man, of things without form and the enslavement of the soul by them, and the divine spirit sent down from heaven to save us. What it was that attracted me in this, what seeds it planted in my stony ground, is still a mystery to me. Yet I can say that, like the legend of the waterfall, this difficult tale was absorbed at some deep level in me, a level involving my emotions more than my intellect. So I came to know the author's name, and started to read what he had written.

I wonder if, of all the experiences that we embark on in this life, there is one more peculiar, more precious and inscrutable than that total absorption in another, private world we call the act of reading. This submission to an exclusive view of life, in sym-

---

* Thomas Mann's *Joseph and His brothers* (*Joseph und seine Brüder*).

pathy with which one willingly rejects anything unrelated to it—what else is this but the mental equivalent of first love? And no matter what the object of this first infatuation may be, it is, for the person concerned, a unique experience which he will never encounter twice.

A total silence filled the room. I took down one volume and then another, looking for those passages whose translation I already had by heart. I then returned the books to the shelf, noticing the marks my slightly dusty fingers had made on them. A faint light came through the window, creating a dull glow on countless leather covers. The books wore their bindings like a mask, lined up in silent ranks. They seemed to have no expectation of being read, rigid in their quiet pride, piled up in places, one upon the other, with the dust.

I breathed in deeply, sniffing the mustiness of that room, and as its atmosphere sank down inside me I wasn't there but elsewhere. I was loitering alone in my father's library, no longer the boy leafing through a book of paintings in my uncle's house, but now a small child standing bewildered below that forgotten, high, smoke-stained ceiling, lost among the shelves of books. If I moved, the floor would make that nervous, rusty creaking sound. The fat reference book over there had turned its scornful gaze on me. The book with the red cover on a shelf nearby winked at me in a friendly way. I darted glances at them, just as I had used to do. I expected to see the door with the broken knob open without any sound at all.

There were footsteps. The teacher had come back, waking me abruptly from my dream. It was decided that I should take out a copy of the magazine *Die Neue Rundschau* which had my writer's autobiography in it. There was an advertisement for his novel *Mario and the Magician* on the first page, a simple-looking sketch of a magician which still expressed the outward absurdity of the person remarkably well; or perhaps I only thought so because it aroused memories of my young uncle who had been so keen on conjuring tricks all those years ago.

There seems to be no end to the various strata of one's memory, to the complexity of the way in which things are buried in it. Even now, at an age when most of what I am relating here has ceased to have any real relevance, I still occasionally recall things from the past that are quite new to me. One example that comes to mind involves a silverfish, and probably took place in my father's library again. I remember finding an odd-looking insect, long and thin, on the edge of a book bound in the old Japanese style. It was so still that I could hardly imagine it running, but when I touched it with my fingertip it made off at an incredible rate and instantly disappeared, leaving just a silvery stain on my finger. I'd never seen an insect like it before, and since it seemed out of place in a library, I decided it was probably an exotic visitor from my mother's room. The stain was so bright I rubbed it off on my trousers, worried that my finger might become poisoned, though feeling a slight pang of bittersweet regret as I did so.

While still a child knowing nothing of books, it seems that huge quantities of them were piling up in one room of my uncle's house, but, for some reason, when I at last learned to read I had no inclination to read them. All I ever did was glance occasionally at the pictures in some of them. Perhaps it was something overbearing in the books that put me off, the feeling that they were best left alone to enjoy their own self-importance.

I'm not sure when I started to read things like fairy tales. What I do know is that I found the experience very confusing, those mermaids, fairies, red candles and so on all running wild inside one's head, so that it made one feel quite dizzy. In fact, I found them such a nuisance that I decided on the spot to give up reading altogether. I used to worry about people who read lots of books, who filled their heads with them. What was the point of it? Their heads must feel heavy all day long. I wondered how they could put up with it.... And yet I often thought about the making of books; not about the people who wrote them, but those who actually put them together—their clothes, the look on their faces as they cut the paper and dyed the bindings. I imagined the pleasure it must give to make a really pretty book, and as I sat there with my back against a pile of them it occurred to me that in my next incarnation I might well appear in book form. I wondered what it would be like to be bound in a certain shape and color, stuck in a corner of the dark library, with no one ever reading me, perpetually holding my breath.

I have one photo of my father. I look at it now and feel intensely sorry for him. His eyes seem so very tired, as if they were craving one thing only, to be allowed to sleep, a peaceful, empty sleep. I doubt if there can be any physical condition more relentlessly cruel and painful than to be forced to keep one's eyes forever open. If my father hadn't spent all his time among his books, if he had ever abandoned them for the simpler pleasures of daily life, then some trace of happiness would have shown in his face. But this he never did, despite the fact that he left little behind to show for his pains, and never managed to attain a secure position in the world of scholarship. The books must have taken him in with their pretensions; their arrogance must have been too powerful to escape. For that reason, I prefer not to open any book nowadays if I can possibly avoid it. They frighten me.

But on that day at school, with the copy of the magazine

I'd just borrowed held carefully under my arm, I presumably walked out into the streets with a dazed and happy expression on my face. The smell of early winter was in the air. A sallow mist had risen some time before, and now covered everything. People walked by with their collars turned up. A pale sun occasionally, almost absentmindedly, broke through, lighting up the surface of the river, which had turned a somber color. In the mist the clusters of low-roofed houses looked like animals grown old and huddled together for warmth. The earth felt hard; it must have already started to freeze deep down. But I was scarcely aware of this as I walked along, preoccupied with the revival of the distant past that had occurred earlier in the day, and thinking how the filling-in of these gaps in my memory might gradually bring into focus the kind of the person I really was. I withdrew into a pleasantly vacant state of mind, and the streets wrapped in their chilly mist only impinged as vague dream images seen in passing.

I found that I had entered a large room full of people sitting on chairs. For a while I couldn't understand what I was doing there, and then I noticed on a dais at the front an electric gramophone, which everyone was quietly listening to. There were people looking upward with their eyes closed, and others with their heads resting on their chests. Each seemed to be indulging in some private ritual of his own, somehow very solemn, yet somehow absurd as well.

I wondered how I had managed to get involved in this concert, but since I'd spied an empty chair I decided to sit down. The music shortly came to an end. People around me started standing up, then sitting down again. All this bustle only made me feel increasingly alone, and conscious, too, of how cold and hard the wooden chair was. Then the room became quiet again, and immediately I was caught up in a sound I knew by heart, a flute, its rise and languid fall. I remembered seeing, as I wandered past it in a daze, the words *Afternoon of a Faun* on the signboard outside the hall, and that accounted for my presence here. So I closed my eyes and dreamed, engaged once more in the self-hypnosis I had practiced as a child, my own private ritual.

I peered into the trembling notes of the music, and there I saw a faun in the shadow of a tree, and he sat up lazily and placed a reed pipe to his lips. Overhead was a canopy of silver-green olive leaves, moving of their own accord. I saw the shining, sacred chariot of fire driven by Helios cross over the heavens, which were like dry, hard blue porcelain. The earth was ancient: stone mountains covered in holes like huge beehives. There was also a primitive forest, the woods of Arcadia full of dark shadows pierced by sunlight through the leaves. I saw a host of nymphs, with slim arms, graceful shoulders, faultlessly smooth, naked bodies. Bright-skinned lizards scuttled in the shade of giant ferns, while on the broad leaf of an agave one golden maybug was trying to move its shards, which had been soaked by the rain. Then swarms of moths flew up and, with flickering wings, surrounded all the nymphs, the animals and plants, and me as well. Their eyes burned enormously, strangely beautiful compound eyes, emerald, gold, and silver.

While still involved in this fantasy, I was aware that it suggested I had seen a naked beauty which I wasn't meant to look at. By a natural process of association, I then began to imagine a scene depicted in an ancient artifact, the birth of the goddess who gave Eros his golden arrows. A wide-ranging sun pours down upon the sea, illuminating a noble, delicate form playing in the waves, a perfect image of its creator's inspiration; and about it

Neptune plies his trident, raising the foam, the flecks and spray of the waves, in a hymn of praise. As the surface of the sea parts in welcome, the four goddesses of the seasons bare the everlasting crown that will be placed upon the head now rising from the water....

The melody of the flute returned again, hesitated, weakened, then fell apart. As I looked out over the sea of heads in front of me, a figure rose among them and started walking in my direction. Dressed in a neat lemon-colored sweater, she moved as gracefully as those nymphs of mine, and—without exaggerating—the sweet, slim shape of her face had something of the beauty of that goddess emerging from the waves. I stared at her in blank astonishment, so closely did she resemble the girl I'd always loved in my imagination. Even her hair was auburn-tinged, and fell softly, carelessly, to her shoulders. She kept her eyes lowered, but there was a suggestion of irritation, even anger, in her expression as she walked past me nibbling at her lower lip; and yet the one glance she gave me from those dark, flashing eyes was enough to thoroughly bewitch me. Nothing in existence could be more attractive, it seemed to me; and if anyone accuses me of overdoing my description of this girl, I can only remind him of my response to the insects in that field at home, which endowed them with a brilliant life and purity not normally thought to exist in the world we know.

She was standing in the entrance to the hall, awkwardly putting on what looked like a man's raincoat she'd been carrying on her arm. To my own surprise I found that I had followed her, and was now watching her, finding her girlish figure even more appealing when wrapped in an old gray mackintosh. She had lowered her dimpled chin and was brushing the dust off the coat. Then she looked up again, her innocent lips forming an ironic half-smile as she glanced at the program on the signboard. She raised her right hand and swept the hair from her pale amber cheeks with her slim fingers, then walked away with a child's neat steps.

The mist still covered the streets. Rows of despondent-looking houses stretched hazily away. The ground was damp though quite hard beneath one's feet. From time to time I felt a stab of emotion inside me, a feeling no clearer to me then than the evening mist drifting over the town. I tried to muffle the sound of my footsteps, to shake off the sense of moving in a trance, and fixed my eyes on the shape walking a short distance ahead of me as if this precious vision might somehow fade from sight. Suddenly the mist parted and a few rays of the dying sun broke through to the street, turning the girl's hair a vivid auburn, and I was lost again in recollections of the past.

I finally caught up with her in the square in front of the station. She was standing waiting for a small old-fashioned streetcar to pass, and I noticed that the cold had brought a flush of color to her cheeks. I took in the thin arch of her eyebrows, the eyes which stared intently though at no fixed point, and the slightly pert, dangerous-looking mouth. It was as if all the various things I'd loved and longed for had returned to me in that one moment, and although her looks had more character than those I'd privately admired, they still conformed to a pattern I recognized.

Once, she glanced at me again, her face looking rather sullen, though it may have been due to the light; and when that suspicious glance had decided to pass me by, I felt a shame and confusion I'd never experienced with such force before, and looked down at my feet. I was uncertain what to do, so I just stood there, until everything in the world began to seem complicated and unhappy (to borrow a phrase from my writer); and I watched the girl, whom I thought I would never see again, disappear inside the station.

Smoke rose into the low, dismal sky behind the station, and I heard the reverberations of the steam engine as it started off. After a little while I realized that I no longer had my copy of *Die Neue Rundschau*, but only felt a mild concern at the thought that I had probably lost it.

* * *

The days passed, and the process was reflected in the near ranges of the Alps as the wind blew the rock faces bare and cumulonimbus clouds floated up from deep among them. Then, quite unexpectedly, my magician uncle sent me a fairly large money order from Kyoto, where he now had a house, and I decided to go on a trip.

The journey was totally unplanned. I simply took a train going north and got off at the first out-of-the-way station that took my fancy, repeating the same process after that. It seemed a fair reflection of my life so far, to travel about like this. In the end, I even reached the stage of not knowing where I was or where the train was taking me.

In a small town in some part of the country, I watched a film which must have been made a generation before. It was a foreign film, very sentimental and peaceful although it broke down in a number of places, and when it was over I joined a crowd of small children watching a picture-story show in the dusty square in front of the station. This passed the time until the next train left. Perched on one of the coaches' steps and simply hanging on (I suppose there must still be people about who remember having to get on and off these packed trains through the windows), I spent a long time watching a monotonous, unfamiliar landscape slide by. There were some low hills, a few paddy fields which soon passed, a number of towns and villages, and finally when night fell a leaden sea behind pine groves, presumably the Japan Sea. I got off at the next small station. It had no enclosure, and only two passengers left the train, myself and a man who reeked of fish. I walked past the few houses toward the sea.

I reached the shore, empty for miles it seemed, with the usual fragrance of the beach mingling with the smell of tar. I walked silently along the sand which overlapped my feet, then sat down in the shadow of a small boat meaning to spend the night there, and thought once more about the past, trying to fit together the fragments that memory had grudgingly unearthed. The black sea swayed peacefully, and under the low night sky, to the accompanying rise and fall of the waves' deep whisper, I went on sorting through these fragile bits and pieces. By this time I had managed somehow to recall practically all the experiences of early childhood described in the first chapter of this tale, either in dreams at night, or stirred by certain delicate smells or unpretentious landscapes; all coming back to life equally mysteriously.

I saw this quest of mine as an attempt to clarify the nature of my own being; not an idle game I played inside my head but a physiological necessity inevitably linked to what I was now, in the flesh. Thus I was able to recall the living beauty of the grasses in the field, the strange shapes of a number of insects, the raw pitch-darkness of the parlor, and some members of my family long since dead. I was also able to understand, if still only imperfectly, that my passionate love of nature took a number of different basic forms. I also understood the relevance of the background to all this, those tombstones in the graveyard, for it was because death surrounded all these things that the images of nature I retained were so affecting. The one thing I didn't understand, however, was why I couldn't remember my mother's face. I knew that I had thought her beautiful when I was small, and I remembered the way she moved and the intonations of her voice, but no matter how hard I tried to summon up the face itself, nothing would come. Often in my dreams I had sensed the vague white form before me, and woken myself up as I stretched out my arms toward it, and that night on the beach I tried the same thing several times; but the pale vision failed to take shape, and all I saw was the endless expanse of dark green waves, all I heard was the quiet groaning of the sea. I moved my cold body a little on the damp sand, feeling again the helplessness of an infant who can do nothing for himself.

Sometimes I slept in cheap boarding houses, but mostly I spent the night in the open air or in a corner of some station platform. It was certainly more comfortable than sleeping on a mountain ridge thousands of feet up, and the cloak that high-school students wore in those days (even in summer) was a real blessing. On some nights, by the light of a naked bulb which insects swarmed about, I read a book by that writer who had already become an inseparable part of me, rereading time and time again those pages where, in the most polished of phrases, he explains how a sense of intimacy with death results in a consciousness of life. There were also certain lines I liked to brood about, lines I knew by heart, as I looked up at the stars.

His various ironies and antitheses concerning the spirit and nature (nature at times meaning just life itself, at times the flesh) were in many cases probably only understood by me in a misguided, superficial way, and were also, to some extent, an affectation; yet they still provided me with ideas that could take emotive shape. Innocence often apprehends irony, not as a means

162

of creating objective distance, but in close, personal terms, and it was a fundamental mistake on my part to see a clear opposition between the spirit and nature, since they are essentially the same, appearing different only when seen from certain angles. The fact that the distinction should have been maintained from ancient times, however, either indicates how essentially man is a creature of both reason and emotion, or suggests at least that our ideas are based much more on the feelings and sensations of childhood than we think. In my case, anyway, various rigid concepts linked to feelings and sensations of that time took firm root in me, and these were of the drastic kind that goes with immaturity, particularly under the stimulus of the rarified air of high alpine peaks. Thus a sort of magic veil was cast over both the spirit and the flesh, blurring their outlines and making them entirely abstract. I decided, for example, that beauty was the only form whereby the spirit could be experienced as physical sensation, that the spirit was incapable of the highest levels of contemplation unless it made use of the flesh, and that God only existed in the things one loved—ideas that were not only very neatly contrived but worthy of the highest form of ridicule; and all very ancient ones, of course, dug up by me with great ceremony, and then accepted with a good deal of innocent enthusiasm.

This led to other flights of fancy, with the result, for instance, that I found myself virtually worshiping all sorts of people in my past for their physical gifts, from my cousin cleverly spinning a plate on a stick and the baseball manager who was somebody after all, to the way my mother and sister looked. There were exceptions, naturally, but I even managed to include some aspects of myself, despite my physical failings. And this, too, presumably was another sign of immaturity—the need to make absolute judgments, to set the seal of approval on what one most admires.

Yet now, looking back, though I can understand the sense of private shame that people often feel about their youth and the ideas that flourished then, I don't entirely share it; for those awkward, unweaned theories of mine, developed on mountaintops, did in fact provide my life, willful and extravagant as it became, with some kind of fixed center, creating a balance it would never have had without them. By this I mean that, whatever ups and downs occurred later on the surface of my life, I seemed to have experienced them already at some deeper level, and of the various things that happened to me none was ever as disturbing as those inner events which took place when there were no problems in the outside world at all.

… I walked down any number of streets. Sometimes when I stopped in places that had been badly bombed, with only a few makeshift huts erected here and there, I remembered the nights I'd spent escaping the flames in Tokyo as if it was all something that had happened very long ago; and I was even more surprised how, at the time, I seemed to have lost any power I might have had to observe things. In all that fire and destruction I should have seen many forms of life and death, but the fact remained that I'd seen nothing. I had stood in a line with other people waiting for a handout of emergency rations—drenched to the skin, with a piece of cloth over one eye which had got a spark in it. While I stood there they were digging open the underground shelters, releasing the stench of scorched flesh as they did so; and yet even the most indifferent bystander would have noticed more than I did. I began to wonder now just how much of that so-called experience, indeed if any of it, had left its mark, and for a moment the thought stirred me a little, but also depressed me to the same extent.

So I mingled with the jostling crowds in the black market,

and enjoyed looking past all these strangers' shoulders at the bits and pieces they had on sale, delighted that there was no chance of anyone suddenly addressing me by name. I had a meal, indulging in the extravagance of using two coupons, then went and sat for a long time on a park bench. After that I leaned on the railing of a bridge, staring at the oily, sluggish water and watching a boat drift by until it disappeared from sight. Like a man in a story I'd once read, who spends each night talking to a woman who appears out of his wardrobe, I said to myself: "This is a river. This is called a river. I don't know what stupid name it's got, and I'd rather not know it."

About three months after I had first met her, I saw the girl again. It was at an exhibition of pictures by a local artist which she had come to with a girl friend. The painter lived at the foot of the Alps and specialized in mountain scenes (drawing nothing else, in fact). The pictures themselves were competent, quite pretty, and completely ordinary. Even so, there were a few landscapes I could stand in front of and relive the way my own eyes had experienced the scenery they depicted. Among them was an oil painting of a valley in early spring, with thick snow still lying in the shadows of the cliffs, and a gentle sunlight on the rocks, the branches, and some muddy water; and as I stood and looked at it I had the peculiar feeling again of rediscovering something precious that I'd lost somewhere. It was, I knew without a doubt, a valley I had sometimes rested in when I made my first excursions into the mountains, for I could recognize the place where I'd broken off a branch to make a walking stick, the spot under a cliff where there was a large ants' nest, and the bank of the stream where I'd sat and bathed a cut on my leg with cold water. But gradually the discrepancies between the way I remembered the valley and this portrayal of it began to bother me, and I moved on to the next picture, to discover that I was standing right next to the slender girl I had never for one moment forgotten.

She didn't look particularly attractive as she stood there talking to the other girl about something totally unrelated to art. I felt no great surprise at seeing her there, either. In fact it seemed perfectly natural, as natural as my recognizing a group of trees in a picture I was looking at. Because I was a little disappointed in her looks, I felt bold enough to stare openly at her profile; and, just as what seems at first an unprepossessing piece of scenery gradually reveals its secrets to an observant person, so her small, neat face began to come alive, to shine, to be radiant, and, before long, my heart was thumping as I realized just how beautiful she was. Here, for me, was the perfect artifact, faultless in every aspect.

She turned her head in an oddly artificial way, and said something to her companion. I could just catch the inflections of her voice, slightly nasal in tone and a little blurred in her final syllables. She walked a few slow steps and raised her left hand slowly to her cheek. The gesture gave the impression she was trying to ward off something. The slim fingers with slightly prominent knuckles passed almost directly in front of my eyes. Her fingernails were untidy, as if she had the nasty habit of biting them, but those round, in places ragged nails looked irresistible to me.

The two girls completed a circuit of the fairly small exhibition room, then sat down together on a bench by the window. There was another room nearby, with a table in the center on which were arranged some pressed leaves from various alpine plants, and seven or eight people were grouped around it. Since it was comparatively dark in there it was an excellent place to hide, so

I mingled with that small crowd in such a way that I could observe the girl face on, with feelings of excited trepidation. While talking to her friend she would sometimes gaze up at nothing in particular, and as she did so her deep black eyes, which to anyone else might have seemed quite ordinary, were for me as different from all the other objects in those rooms as anything could be. And my own eyes, hidden though they were behind other people's backs, lost their nerve, and looked elsewhere. So I watched nervously as the winter sunlight, pale and hesitant, lit up that bench under the window, showing me those sweet, delicate features.

It was a perfect parody of the relationship between "the spirit" and "life": me standing unseen in the shadows watching her, a paragon, in the sunlight, and my heart ached at the thought that I was destined to remain an onlooker, anonymous and unnoticed, my face showing the strain that my spirit was enduring. I wondered whether there wasn't some way I could approach her, even exchange a few words with her, but it was quite impossible because I knew that the two girls spoke a different language, living as they did in the bright light of the everyday....

I admit that my distress was really rather ludicrous, but I look back on it now with some affection and respect, seeing it as a good example of the absurdity of youth itself (assuming that youth is actually absurd).

After that I met the girl a number of times, completely by accident. Since we were both living in the same, not particularly large, town, I suppose one could say it wasn't all that strange; yet it certainly seemed so to me because each episode was so indefinite, as vague as the mist in which the streets were wrapped and behind whose veil she seemed inevitably more mysterious, arousing an even deeper longing in me.

These chance encounters were much like those I'd had in childhood with butterflies whose names I didn't yet know: the blue butterfly, *Canessa canace*, with its fitful, phosphorescent glow, or the *Danaus tytia*, as graceful as a sylph. I knew where these butterflies were to be found, but never actually seemed to find them when I went to seek them out with net in hand; and then one would suddenly appear, high up on a cliff where I couldn't reach it, or at a moment when I happened to be strolling along without my net. It was in the same way that I met the girl occasionally, and each time she seemed different, perhaps because of the weather or the clothes she was wearing, or more likely because some slight shift in her feelings that day was reflected in her soft, fragrant skin. On these occasions I felt I was observing the same kind of infinite variations one sees in identical species of insects in the same mountainous area as they change with the passing season.

I saw her one day when it was snowing, wearing an overlarge gauze mask over her nose and mouth, which made her look even more helplessly charming. Each breath she took turned into tiny drops of water which clung to her long eyelashes, and snowflakes were caught in her hair, loose and blowing in the wind. Then, in the sunlight of early spring, I watched her playing with her friends, frisking about like a young animal. Once I saw her with her thick hair blown back from her forehead by the hot south wind of summer, and as she walked forward leaning into it she looked up at me for a moment, and those upturned, sparkling black eyes of hers seemed then very far indeed from my idea of "the spirit." As the weather had got warmer, more of her body was revealed, and I saw the slender nape of her neck, the slim arms, all the youthfulness of her figure. And just as in the past, when staring at the neck of another girl getting on a bus, I watched her in a crowd of memories.

Yet none of this meant I was able to get any closer to her. I never once thought of speaking to her. Even though my firmly held theory on the subject of the spirit and the flesh seemed to insist on it, there was something still more positive in me that held me back. After all, each time I'd ever made a conscious approach toward any of those forms of beauty which had attracted me before, hadn't they all immediately disappeared from sight?

Meanwhile, I was still continuing my travels, spending several days and nights away each time. One day I turned up at my magician uncle's house in Kyoto, an unplanned visit like all the others. He got drunk on the month's ration of saké, then showed some of his old brilliance with the trick of drawing multicolored handkerchiefs out of his fist. But though it made me sentimental to some extent about the past, I found this in itself aroused a certain sense of estrangement, and I took the train back the next day. I had to return to school for the end-of-term exams anyway.

At Nagoya I changed to the Central Line, and since there was some time before my connection I wandered around the town a bit, getting back to the station in the evening when it was swarming with travelers and tramps. A number of grubby little boys were hanging about the queues of passengers, begging food off them, and others were sleeping in groups, piled almost one on top of the other, by the station pillars. They were so soundly asleep I felt a pang of envy; envious also of their freedom, as I thought with distaste of the various ties that bound me to the world. I'd been thinking about such things ever since I got on the train at Kyoto, and this had only accelerated the process. So I decided to consult a certain lady I knew about it all, even if it did mean suddenly bursting in on her.

I didn't really know her, in fact, at all. After another point-lessly hectic day toward the end of the war, I had returned to my uncle's house just as a visitor was being shown out, and that was the first and last I'd seen of her. We were getting ready to evac-uate the house, and there was straw matting and rope all over the floor of the entrance hall, and this elegantly kimonoed lady was stepping over it when she noticed me and turned back to my aunt to ask her something, speaking too quickly for me to catch her question. Just one glance, however, was enough to make me extremely nervous, for I had the odd feeling it was probably my mother. But she looked at me very calmly, and two or three words quickly dispelled this notion. I don't remember what we talked about, perhaps because nothing memorable was said, but I soon felt completely at ease with her. She then made the usual parting remarks to us, and left. It was only later that I found out quite by accident that she had known my parents well when they were living abroad.

So when her name was mentioned at my young uncle's house I immediately remembered that episode. Her husband had spent much more time abroad than in Japan before the war, and had known my father ever since he first went to Europe. My uncle said the lady would be pleased to see me, and he wrote down her address for me, suggesting I send her a letter.

Thus I took a different train to the one going home. Luckily I was able to find a seat. My destination was five or six stations away, and I sat there in a state of some suspense, which wouldn't let me settle down for quite a while.

* * *

When dinner was over the atmosphere of the room became

170

heavily lethargic. It seemed particularly so to me, since I was not only bloated with food but also fairly drunk on some whisky which I wasn't used to, a condition I found half unpleasant and half unreal. I sat slumped against the back of my chair, engaged in a constant effort to make some sense out of the blurred objects around me. The European style of the room was difficult to adjust to, particularly for someone who had lived through the war. And yet I also had a strange sense of having reencountered things known long ago, like a kind of homecoming. The ivory ornaments on the shelves, the pieces of majolica, the Gobelin tapestry on the wall, even the Sphinx, the pyramids, and the laden camels on that tapestry, all inspired such feelings.

The table had not yet been cleared. The lady had gone to a great deal of trouble to provide me with rare things to eat, and I had put away everything placed in front of me with such alacrity that her daughter, a delightful girl of about twelve or thirteen, finally couldn't restrain her laughter; and even the mother smiled and said my performance was like a conjuring trick. Her words had a melancholy ring to them as they died away, and I noticed how similar her daughter's way of speaking was, particularly on one occasion when, after being scolded for giggling and playfully criticized for being so greedy herself, she had covered her face and whispered something I couldn't quite make out, until I realized that she'd been speaking in German, probably asking her mother to stop. The words had such a dying fall I wasn't all that sure she had actually said them, thinking perhaps I was hearing things; but her mother then told me the girl still had the habit of talking occasionally in the language she'd used as a small child abroad.

On hearing this, the girl pretended she didn't know what her mother was talking about, assuming an expression of unconcern which made her look all the more childlike, and I felt I could see in her what my sister would have become if she had lived. It wasn't surprising I had thought of her, for the foreign atmosphere of this house was something I'd already experienced at home, down to the Sèvres plates on the table and the square bottle of whisky with its black label. This was, in fact, the world of my mother; the room was redolent of her, and I opened my eyes and looked alternately at these two who now shared that world with her, and were the same kind of person. I found the idea extremely moving, and this emotion was only reinforced when the girl precariously placed a record on the old-fashioned gramophone, becoming so powerful I was forced to lower my head as I heard again the tones of that flute to which I had grown so accustomed. I didn't know whether it had been chosen for me on purpose or not.

When the music came to an end and only the sound of the needle scratching on the still revolving record could be heard, the lady asked me if I liked it, and I nodded.

"I wonder if you remember?" she asked in a vague manner. Then, after a longish pause, she added as though she were talking to herself, "Your mother used to like it so much."

In my intoxication I was able to remember and understand: the bright-lit scene in the parlor, bursts of talk and laughter here and there among the assembled guests, the tinkle of glasses, myself sitting alone in a corner; and then my mother, at the center of it all, bending low over the impressive boxlike gramophone and turning the handle. Yet was it indeed this music? And was this the reason why it had always attracted me? I closed my eyes, seeming to watch an old-fashioned revolving lantern as it creaked around, showing one ancient picture after another, yet all become new again. Only my mother's face remained a blank.

At last it was time for the girl to go to bed. Her mother took her to the door, where she looked back at me and smiled sleepily, giving her mother a light embrace and being kissed on her slightly artificial-looking hair in return. All this also was as it had been in the past, and my dead mother and sister were both wonderfully alive again before my eyes. As the girl's footsteps died away the silence came back at once; a languid, if rather prickly sort of silence.

"You don't seem to have deliberately battered your cap like the usual high-school student," the lady said after a while, as though trying to pick up a thread in the interrupted conversation, looking over at my cap with its white stripe hanging there on the wall. I replied quite seriously that the contents of my head were so peculiar I at least needed some decent, ordinary covering for them, and as I said this I remembered the odd conversations I'd had with the medical student, and almost felt like giggling. She continued with more inquiries about my student life, but was apparently disappointed to hear no account of ragging in the dorm or other fun and games she associated with being young, to the point where she couldn't help asking me eventually, in a puzzled-sounding voice:

"Then what exactly do you do?"

"Me? Well, I don't know. Mountain climbing, I suppose."

"You must read a lot of books?"

"Yes—ones about the Martians, mainly."

I immediately regretted making such a conversation-stopping reply. The lady was much older than I had imagined her to be: her hair, which was slightly untidy, had already lost its luster, and there were signs of weariness at the corners of her eyes and mouth, although the still bold, large eyes were generous and kind.

"Do you think you could tell me something about life abroad?" I suddenly blurted out.

"Abroad?" she repeated, looking at me questioningly. "You mean about your ... ?"

"Yes," I interrupted her. "I want to know. I'm old enough to."

I spoke impatiently, but I was worried that if I didn't speak out now I might not get another opportunity. So I told her everything, everything I knew, everything I remembered. Whenever I paused for a moment I could feel the night outside pressing in to fill the empty spaces. Finally I had finished, and as I closed my mouth, tiredness seemed to weigh down on my forehead.

"I feel so sorry for you," she said, as if she thought it had been tactless on her part to mention my mother in the first place; but she went on: "You certainly seem to remember your old home very well, though, considering how small you were at the time."

"I know. But I'd forgotten it all completely. When I was at middle school I went back once to try and find it, but I had no idea where it was, where the house was at all. Only when I walked past the cemetery, then I seemed to feel something, but that's all."

"What happened after that?"

"Well, after moving up to Matsumoto, I began to remember things gradually. Then I went back to Tokyo for the first time at the beginning of last summer and made up my mind to find the house, feeling somehow excited, afraid, and embarrassed all at the same time, but when I got there the whole of that area had been burned down. There were only a lot of temporary huts. I just had to give up.

"I gave up and went to the cemetery instead. That at least hadn't changed. I can still clearly remember how I wandered for

174

hours among the gravestones and the hedges, half convinced I knew what I was looking for, and half aware that I didn't. It was a funny feeling, almost as if this wasn't really happening and I was only dreaming it. Then I came to an enormous camphor tree. The trunk was covered with a plant called a hare's-foot fern, and it was so big it would have taken four children at least to link arms around it. As I felt the bark of that old tree with my hands, I closed my eyes, and could see myself running through the maze of tombstones I'd played in when I was small. When I opened them, the scene was just the same as before. I enjoyed doing this a few more times, then lay down in the grass where the cemetery joined the field.

"I don't know if you know of a plant—just a weed, in fact—that's got a sap like iodine, which comes out when you break off the stem; anyway, there was some of that growing there. Plenty of mosquitoes about, as well. Then I moved slightly for some reason, and smelled something that was so familiar it made me cry out in surprise. The smell seemed to spread right through me, and suddenly it all came back to me, everything about the old house, what the hallway was like, the furniture in the parlor, the dark staircase, all sorts of things all at the same time. I got up and looked at the plant that had been brushing against my head. It was groundsel. The whole field used to be covered in it. At least I'm fairly certain it was."

There was the sound of something knocking against the window, and we both looked up. It was a large, pale blue emperor moth, its wings throbbing as it tried to get in.

"What's that?" the lady asked.

"A large silk moth. *Actias artemis*."

"*Actias artemis*," she repeated. "You're just like your father—full of unusual bits of information."

Her voice was barely a murmur, fading at the end, and I realized it was getting late. But after a few moments of silence she inquired hesitantly if I would like to see some photos, and produced an old, worn leather album, so ancient one expected the smell of mildew to rise from its pages. My hands were trembling when I took hold of it. I opened the thick cover and looked at the pictures, yellow and faded with age, of scenes abroad: narrow streets crammed with gabled houses, squares with high Gothic fountains, a dark, swift-flowing river with a cathedral on the far bank, which was the Danube in Vienna, as she explained while looking at them with me.

"Where's this?"

"It's a town called Lübeck in northern Germany. We once spent a fortnight there."

An inexplicable sense of warmth arose in me, gradually filling my whole body; an excitement apparently restricted to me alone. I made a few confused remarks and heard her mechanical replies.

"Yes, most of the architecture in the cities of the Hanseatic League was in this style."

"Was there a house called Buddenbrooks?"

"I'm almost sure there was. Probably that very old house just off the main street."

"Do you think it's still there?"

"It's hard to say. I did ask someone who'd just got back recently, and it does seem the bombing wasn't too bad there. Only the town center got hit.... But why are you so interested?"

I was about to reply, but instead simply swallowed and turned the page.

"Do you recognize her? That's your mother."

I stared at the picture as though examining an object of great mystery, and saw a small, slender girl standing in front of what appeared to be a castle, with a beret pulled low on her forehead, and looking in a rather dazzled way toward the camera. But this was a youngish girl, not my imagined mother but more like what I would have expected my sister to become; more like this lady's daughter, in fact, and perhaps most of all like the girl whose name I didn't know and who had aroused all those secret torments in me.

"It's a town called Rottenburg, with quite a medieval atmosphere to it still. Your mother lived there a long time and often said it was the place she had the fondest memories of. No, I was given this some time after it was taken. I was in Japan, you see, by then. In fact it was much later; your father gave it to me when I first saw him again here. No, I'm afraid all the later photographs were burned…. Such a pity, because your father had masses of them…."

She began to talk, pausing frequently, about her memories of the past. I listened in silence. Any desire to ask questions had vanished now, and I simply listened to what she had to say, making sure I remembered every word. After what seemed like quite a long time, she finally broke off and asked me, in a playful tone of voice as though trying to cheer me up, if I really disliked studying all that much. I was lost for a reply, so she went on:

"I must say I'd find it rather amusing if you did, as I could never quite work out if your father was really as wrapped up in his books as everybody thought he was, or whether he wasn't just being very lazy in a deliberately energetic sort of way."

"Lazy in an energetic way?"

"Yes. For example, if we went to a museum together he would just fold his raincoat, put it on the floor, then sit on it and scribble in his notebook. He'd pay no attention to us at all, either glaring fiercely at a picture or sitting with his eyes closed, so we would go around by ourselves, and when we came back he would be exactly the same, quite oblivious of his surroundings. Of course, he'd then notice what had been going on, and get very cross with himself; get in such a huff, in fact, that he'd refuse to look at any of the other paintings and rush out of the place, as though leaving the scene of a crime. It was too funny for words."

I laughed as well; but I also felt I knew him more intimately now, this father who had died before I'd had a chance to get acquainted with him.

It was well past midnight. The visitors at the window had folded their wings and were quiet now. We said goodnight to each other. I wondered if I hadn't had a conversation like this before, one similarly aimless and made up of words like those one hears when dreaming deeply. But with whom or when I didn't know.

Unable to sleep that night, I brooded over the various facts and images encountered during the day, all of which had been absorbed like water on dry soil, things different in meaning from what I'd learned from the mountains over the past two years. Among them I recalled a drawing I happened to have made, and the response it aroused in the lady's daughter. It was sometime in the afternoon, and, having nothing much to do, I'd picked up some pastels and paper that had been left lying around. The mother was preparing dinner; the only sound in the unfamiliar room was the ticking of the clock. At first I just added lines and colors to each other at random, but at some point I realized I was in fact tracing a particular shape, an image I was unable to remember with any precision yet couldn't easily forget. It was an almost formless white object against a dark background, but the darkness itself was an elaborate combination of various shades, which seemed alive and writhing on the page.... I heard a sound behind me, and turned to find it was the daughter, who must have just got home from school since she was dangling her satchel in one hand as she looked inquisitively at my sketch. She didn't seem shy at all, and the animation in her face prompted me to behave as if we'd know each other for some time. I asked her if she knew what it was. She nodded.

"Yes. It's a G,H,O,S,T."

As she spelled out her reply, I was amazed that what I'd drawn meant something to another person.

"A ghost? How do you know that? Have you ever seen one?"

She laughed, not in the way one does to please a guest, but because she thought the question funny.

"I've seen them in dreams."

"Were you frightened?"

"No. They're not frightening. Mummy told me there's nothing to be frightened of."

"What were the ghosts, then? What kind of ghosts did you see?"

"I don't know. You see, ghosts don't really exist. It's all just something going on inside your head."

"Just inside your head?"

"That's what Mummy says. Sometimes ghosts actually get inside people and possess them, but that only happens to very unhappy people, she said, people you have to feel sorry for. She says she feels sorry for you."

The girl laughed again. It sounded as if something was tickling her throat.

"Well, it's certainly true that I see ghosts in my dreams."

"Do you really?" she said, looking at me with round, unblinking eyes which seemed alight with various colors, perhaps because the whites had a blue tinge to them. They seemed to regard me with a certain pity....

I was at last beginning to feel sleepy, although the photos of foreign landscapes and my mother as a girl kept drifting through my mind. I saw the cobbled lane with its gabled roofs as if it were a place I'd once known well. For some reason I convinced myself that my father had been walking along that road, his back slightly stooped, when he had met the pretty girl who was to become my mother.

Finally I fell into a light sleep, and a few hesitant, wistful dreams soothed me as I slept. The image I had drawn appeared as well—dim and distant, but no stranger to me—though when my eyes opened all I saw was that I was in bed in someone else's house, and that the darkness was tinged with the pale light of approaching dawn.

* * *

Quite by accident, at the end of summer, something extraordinary happened to me. In any life there seem to be one or two experiences that are clearly predestined; and if fate really does have a hand in human life, then my own experience of the natural world on that occasion can be considered, surely, as something already inherent in me, in my blood, from the very beginning.

I have known numerous kinds of mist: the low mist of dawn slowly filling a valley; the evening mist that comes out of nowhere on a high plateau; the mist of fine rain that clings to the branches of the hemlock fir and the strands of Spanish moss; the mist in a deep gorge which gradually disappears with the rays of the sun. Once, as it drifted over a withered moor, it seemed to touch each frosted blade of grass one by one, so that I almost thought it made a tiny sound each time it did so. Another time, on a mountain pass, the mist was so thick that at each pace I took the trunk of one more tree was revealed, but only one; and that experience was to me just like the process of memory, one image after another appearing by accident from behind the thick curtain of forgetfulness.

Yet the mist I was confronted with on this occasion was of a much more frightening kind, the sort of deep fog only found in the high mountains; and I was enveloped in something as thick as a wall, though it was constantly moving. It lay above and all around me, and below were only the hard gray rocks, with sometimes a rusty boulder through whose cracks the fog poured like a living force. Only the rocks themselves were silent and still.

I was tired. When people start to feel fatigue they become more conscious of their bodies, and, as the tiredness increases, one's sense of physical reality itself becomes ambiguous. I placed my foot on the edge of a rock and it suddenly felt weightless, like walking on a cloud. Again and again I had the sensation of moving in a fog-bound dream. Then a sudden blast of wind blew a hole in the fog, and my head cleared with it. I looked back from the crag on which I was standing, and far above me was a huge crest of rock, and the land that sloped down from there to the valley below was strewn with broken boulders, a weird and violent world of stone. The dense clouds of fog were being blown upward at great speed, until they broke against that far-off peak, immediately concealing it from sight, then just as suddenly revealing it again, as in some sleight of hand. Now the whole side of the mountain, as far as the eye could see, lay exposed, rock upon rock in rigid waves, and all completely silent, drowned in a sinister calm, a total absence of sound as if this world had for-gotten what it was. The only movement in that dead sea of stone and mist was the beating of my pulse.

The fog returned. This landscape like the cold volcanoes of the moon was fading visibly before me. The distant peak clouded over, was now unseen, although the crag nearby was still there; but that soon went, and in no time the thick gray wall was flow-ing all around me, and I had to get a move on, quick, stumbling a few paces over pebbles, then losing my balance, falling, and landing heavily on my thigh.

Where was the snow valley? I should be there by now. What time was it? Late afternoon? Evening? No, it must be night al-ready. Back there near the rocky peak, only the white disk of the sun had appeared when the sky was clear, dropping over the edge of the world, falling into the mist that linked the high mountains. And that, surely, was sunset, wasn't it? As I picked my way mechanically down through the rocks on the steep slope, that was all I could think about. I fell occasionally, and then sat on a rock to recover, feeling a sense of dread steal over me.

I decided I must be dreaming after all. This was an extinct volcano on the moon, and I was the only creature left alive, and soon I too would sink to the ground, and my body would grow cold.... But I refused to believe it. My mind was still alert; I was able to analyze and understand my situation. The black crest I'd seen rising toward the sky was Mt. Yarigadake, in the Northern Alps, and this rock-strewn slope led down to the marshland of Yarizawa, an area well known to me, almost like a public park if compared to regions deeper in the mountains. I was tired, and I hadn't eaten anything since breakfast, that was all. The idea that I was lost was ridiculous. Admittedly, I very nearly had been two days ago, but I'd managed to get myself out of that, hadn't I? My first priority now was—not to find the path again or a place to sleep—but to get enough snow to boil up some rice with at a mountain hut, which I knew wasn't far away.

I'd entered the mountains exactly four days earlier. At first it was all very casual, just wandering about as I pleased. I met no other hikers on the way. On the second day I got lost on a ridge, and soaked to the skin, but managed to reach a climbers' hut before nightfall. There was nobody there. The short climbing season was over, and since the war had only just ended the place was closed and all the bedding had been removed, so I spent the night there shivering with cold. It was pouring with rain in the morning. To make matters worse, I seemed to have a temperature, and found it hard to get up. My food supply was getting low, but I ate a little boiled rice and water, and spent another miserably cold and pitch-dark night in the hut, perched up there on a mountain ridge, miles from civilization. Then, the next day, I found a path I recognized, and more or less followed it to get this far....

Meanwhile, my legs felt as heavy as lead—I couldn't go on—so I sat down on the roots of a creeping pine. Before long, I began to see illusions. A thin face I remembered well, with shining eyes, appeared, one side of it clouded with a certain sadness, the other smiling slightly. Not shy, and yet apparently remote, and tilted a little at one corner, it was the same inscrutable smile as I'd once seen on the face of the girl whose name I didn't know. The smile had been directed at me, at me alone.

It happened at the station just before I set out on this expedition. I was standing on the platform with my rucksack on my shoulders, and I saw her lean out of a window in the train that was waiting there. A number of people had gathered by the window, and a man in Japanese dress who seemed to be her father was passing a large trunk in to her. I realized immediately that the girl was leaving this part of the country, going away to some far-off place, and that an image which belonged in dreams but had come to life in her for the past six months was now about to disappear from sight. I had always known, however, that this was bound to happen, a departure I'd expected from the very start. So I gazed at this cheerful-looking girl who seemed so unaware of me, as she raised one slender, short-sleeved arm to brush her soft hair with its auburn tints away from her forehead. Then, while she was talking and laughing with the people there to see her off, she suddenly turned and looked in my direction. Perhaps she remembered the face of this high-school boy she had seen a number of times. For a while she kept her pretty head in this position, and perhaps for that reason it seemed that she was smiling at me. And there on the platform I recalled another face, the face of the girl being taken away from the factory in a lurching truck, and I felt I must see this passenger off in the same way until she faded out of sight. But I had my own train to catch, which was leaving from a different platform, and, whether deliberately or not, I found my legs moving toward the stairs. My heavy rucksack, shaking about as I walked along, helped to disguise the heaving in my heart.... And while I climbed those mountain paths, now empty with the season over, it was that fleeting image which pursued me, being with me even when I lost my way and was in danger of my life, for which it may have been responsible.

I finally reached the mountain hut, only to discover that it, too, had been closed up and—worse—had no supply of water. Exhausted as I was, I would have to clamber down over the cold gray rocks and somehow try to find my way through the evening mist now rising from the valleys, down to one of the strips of snow that ran toward the marshland I could see opening out below. But much more snow had remained this year than usual, and there was a place only about ten, at the most fifteen, minutes away, a long ribbon of still unmelted snow. I was in a hurry, desperate for something to eat, so I picked up an empty paraffin can I found in the hut and, sliding down a slab of rock on an iron chain which almost froze my hands off, I set off down the rugged slope....

I began to wonder just how long it was since I'd left the hut. It felt as if twenty or thirty minutes, perhaps even an hour, had passed. My watch had stopped two days before. I peered around in the fog, but could make no sense out of its swirling movements. The fact that night had fallen long ago was all I could understand from my surroundings ... night, lying vast and deep across this barren waste, and now inviting me even further in, to share its dream of ice and cold. I felt a numbness creeping up my hands and feet.... I stirred, and found to my surprise that I was squatting on a rock, with a tongue of dirty snow reaching out in front of me.

The fog was still there, turbid but moving quietly now. For a while I couldn't make out what I was doing in this place, why I was surrounded by this mist, why the snow should shine so coldly and stretch so far. I stepped gingerly onto it, and the icy air rose through its seams to bring me slowly to my senses. I took the paraffin can clumsily out of my rucksack, and started scratching at the surface with my bare hands and the lid of my mess tin. The stuff had frozen as hard as stone; but once I'd scraped away the dirty surface, I found a layer of coarse white crystals underneath. My torn fingertips hurt, but eventually I stopped feeling the pain.

Perhaps I was still half asleep after all. The splinters of snow made my eyes water, but I felt some satisfaction as I threw each bit into the can, remembering vaguely a distant time when I had done the same kind of thing in a corner of the field, by a tumbledown brick building where we'd picked up pieces of grayish white hewn stone and busily rubbed away to turn them into powder; and when enough had been made we would put it on leaves and offer it to each other as food. It seemed incredible to me, impossible indeed, that I couldn't see my sister beside me, crouched down pointlessly scraping at a stone, and laughing, as if something was tickling her throat.

A long time seemed to have gone by, and the paraffin can was more than half full. I shouldered it like a sleepwalker, and set off back the way I'd come. I couldn't immediately make out the rocks in front of me, as the mist was much thicker than it had been. Where was I going? Of course I was going back to the hut, but all my attention was focused on my next foothold on a ledge of rock, on keeping my balance. Each step took my breath away. However much I strained my eyes, all I could see was the fog and the night, and I could hear nothing except the sounds I made myself. But I went on laboriously moving my arms and legs, knowing that if I stopped I would never climb the slope, though it gave me no sense of nearing my destination, or even the assurance that I was really moving upward at all. It was like walking in a trance, an experience I also remembered from the past, when lost in the maze of the cemetery; and now too there was a huge tombstone leaning over me, and at my side a crowd of wooden tablets shutting out the world, and all the graves and the paths were ones I'd never seen before; and in front of me was another cluster of tombstones staring at me with their cold faces, blocking my way, and on all sides, between the trees and graves, the thick coils of night reached out, raising their heads and crawling low across the ground toward me....

For some time I had been aware of a vague white shape drifting ahead of me. In the darkness, in the fog, it seemed to be waiting there, a ball of mist perhaps yet moving gently on ahead, beckoning, inviting; and instinctively I followed it. Occasionally a wave of sleep passed through my bone-tired body, making everything seem about to fade. I could feel the familiar hand of death on me again, coldly at my collar and my throat. Sunk deep in ancient dreams, in recollections of the buried past, in a sequence where time seemed at a standstill, I bent one knee and then the other, I clung to each rock in turn, I strained my eyes, keeping that dim shape constantly in sight. It was her. It was the face I had never been able to remember.

She was standing just over there above me, standing on a staircase in darkness, her whole form a hazy white. Yet the hair hanging down over her shoulders, the extraordinarily dark eyes, even the expression on her face, I could see quite clearly. She smiled at me, a sad, rather weary, nervous smile, then made a gesture as if she had understood everything, accepted everything, moving her hand slightly up and down two or three times, her thin fingers stirring the dark air like a swimmer's. I opened my mouth, straining for the word, and when I said it I heard it echoing in my ear, and only then did I know that I had called out to my mother, as I seemed to be falling, falling through the hours, through the days and years.

The numbness gradually subsided in my body; I felt my head suddenly become as clear and cold as ice; and time picked up its usual steady pace again. My tiredness, though, and the pain in my joints returned as well, making me aware again of how chilly the night air was. But the process was completed by my noticing, with a shock, that the stone on which I'd been sitting overlooked a cliff; and I stood up, turning my back on the void below and looking up the mountainside.

At first I couldn't believe what I saw—it seemed beyond belief. Here, ten thousand feet above the sea, a miracle of sorts had taken place, a total transformation of what had been before, a sight spread out around me which inspired an almost mystic sense of awe. Where had the thickly swirling fog vanished to? The sea of mist had ebbed away, and black peaks appeared in it like islands. The sky overhead was without a trace of cloud, sprinkled with a host of stars, and now high above the fog sinking down the slope toward the marshland and the lake below an enormous moon was rising, shimmering white, unnerving, like the approach of an unknown planet. Closer at hand, I saw Ōyari's spearhead shape thrust into the blue-black of the night. The moonlight played on the countless rocks around me, distorting them with freakish-looking shadows.

Only some kind of magic could have produced this change of scene in so brief a space of time, and I leaned against a rock, trying to understand, and gazing in amazement at the mystery of the constellations in their fixed order in the sky. Above me were bright Vega and Altair, on either side of the Milky Way, while slightly to the east that diadem shining bluish white must be Deneb in the Cygnus. Even further east was the W sign of Cassiopeia, the Ethiopian empress, proud of her beauty, with her daughter Andromeda now rising. I looked to the west, and there was the cluster of the Coma Berenices faintly flickering as they declined, and that yellowish-red light must come from Arcturus. In the southern sky Scorpio stretched out its twisted form, and Antares seemed mysteriously to breathe red fire; while the Milky Way unfurled in all its glory, the pathway of the gods summoned

by Jupiter and hastening to attend him at his palace in the heavens.

The unbroken trance still held me in its grasp, as I swung my
head around the arc of this great spectacle, unblinking, and probably ashen-faced. I knew now that I was living in a world of
myth, unconscious of the world below. And I thought of the Creation, the most basic myth of all, by which the other myths sus-
tained their being. In the beginning was only chaos, a formless
world of swirling, shifting fog. Chaos gave birth to the earth and
to night, and from the egg of night love was born. These three
things were there from the beginning of life.... And now the
gray earth, these linked crests of rock, had grown quiet, covered
by a dark blue night which looked as if it might absorb them all.
Earth was this row of soaring, black, yet still familiar peaks, mere
shapes of pointed stone above the ever-sinking mist; but in my
eyes it was also something else, the mountains of Olympus where
the gods were served by Hebe, and raised their cups. Apollo,
wrapped in his flowing robe, played the lyre, and to that melody
the Muses sang....

I was startled by the sound of a rock falling from near the top
of Mt. Ōyari, bounding several times with a harsh, metallic ring,
and thus emphasizing the silence that returned as the echoes
faded. In the perfect solitude it left behind, I felt I could still hear
the faint sounds made by the spirits of the hills, whose leader,
Echo, lives in caves, in valleys and cliffs, and only speaks when
called to by a human voice; and I felt she was now hiding there
in the shadow of that fallen rock.

With my head bent slightly to the left, absorbed in my clumsy
thoughts, I sat there as if turned to stone in the moon's cold light
which still lay over this desolate scene. I had the feeling that

189

something was on the verge of being born; that the egg of night would soon secretly split open, and the final myth emerge. And just as I thinking this, a gleam of light I'd only been aware of unconsciously till then appeared as two eyes, which aroused in me a strange embarrassment. After them came locks of hair, a neck, the whole shape itself, appearing only momentarily and with no apparent purpose, but still undeniably there. And I felt this must be the god who lives in the shadow of the summit beyond, that sweet god who will never grow old, the son of Venus who shoots the arrows of desire; and he was about to approach me, laughing to himself....

Another rock fell, a more startling sound this time, high-pitched and shrill, sending a shiver through my spine as it echoed down the slope, yet also finally fading into silence. And so normality returned. I readjusted my rucksack on my back, and by the light of the moon made my way between the piles of stone, uncertainly, stumbling sometimes, climbing up toward the hut.

It was so cold I couldn't sleep, and spent most of the night in the darkness of the hut watching the wavering flames of a small fire I'd made on the earthen floor from a few chips of wood. I was not only worn out but still exalted by the episode outside; yet there was also a feeling of disillusionment spreading through me. It was like the sense of awakening I'd experienced on that mountain when I first came to these parts, but this was more intense, a much drier sensation, a settled, hard awareness of my own solitude.

I went outside the hut, and the night sky, more beautiful than ever, hung in eternal stillness over the black chain of peaks, and the grand constellations continued their relentless pilgrimage, infinitely slow in pace and yet unerringly changing their assured positions, while each fixed star maintained its station, quietly glinting, quivering, with sometimes a falling star slipping between them.

Then, as can only happen in the high mountains at the dead of night, I heard—standing numb with cold, in the center of that silence—a low reverberation, sounding like the spirits of the mountains calling in the distance, words of that ancient language which existed when men and nature were still as one. And the electricity of the earth and the sky answered one another, as I saw, from out of a mass of cloud extending from a deep valley to the middle sky, a twisted flicker of lightning flash and climb. With each burst of light the sea of cloud lit up, the black peaks shone, the shadow passed from off the stardust in the heavens.

Yet all this was so distant, so pure, so unconnected with myself. The more I looked, the more remote it seemed from human life; and even if this distance was a source of deep unhappiness in our lives, it was still a fact, and one that in my heart could no longer be denied. The stars trembled, the rocks slept in their own silence, the cloud stagnated in the valleys, and the coldness of the air seeped through my clothes. So the desire to be with others of my kind welled up in me, the will to go down into the lower world where men had made their homes, as soon as the dawn had come. This urge seemed fixed in me, with a firmness which none of those things I'd felt and thought so far—my various undeveloped theories and ideas—had ever had. And at last a hint of change came into the sky as, with the moon already hidden a while before, the brightness of the stars began to dim, and the faintest tinge of light started to filter through the blackness of the night. And so, as it had done for me so many times before on these solemn mountaintops, after a long, uncertain wait, the dawn broke. As the sun rose, the mist, withdrawn deep inside the folds below, poured forth again, and in no time at all its icy air was eddying about my head, with its bitter, iron smell.

When I finally left the hut some bright rays of sunlight had broken through, showing me the heaps of stone and shining on the remaining patches of snow. I clambered over rocks, I eased my way between them, going down now, always down, back to the world below. The late-flowering alpine plants, already past their prime, started to appear and then increase where I walked, and a reddish satyrid butterfly, which I must have woken up, fluttered into the air and passed me, hurrying on its way.

Now I only had one thought in mind: to go down to join the rest of mankind. It was even possible that sometime, somewhere, I might meet that girl again, even though now she was no longer any special individual, but a shadow image, as I saw it, of my mother as she was when young, or my sister as she would have been. In the same way that my father had met my mother all those years ago in a foreign country, so I, too, might find her again, and thus find perhaps all those things, buried in me from the beginning of my life, revealed in their true clarity. No doubt it was a foolish dream, but one that I regard as sacred.

The path was now through larches and wildflowers. I saw clusters of pink cranesbill and a few butterflies which had survived the end of summer, but they were like beggars with their clothes all ragged and torn. I heard the sound of my breath, the tramp of my boots on the rocks. It was the true sound of the mountains, the resonance of that limitless expanse of stone, of the great earth sounding its message to men as it had done from the very beginning; and it echoed in me like fate itself.

And certainly, if there is such a thing as fate, and if indeed it truly does exist within our blood, informing what we are and what we do; then what could be less mysterious than that it should take that form, that it should sound from out of the heart of the natural world, the true mother of our being?